W9-ABT-447

"How can we be married?"

"Easily. You said the vows, as did I."

"But if I didn't know what I was doing, if I didn't *realize*, surely it can be annulled?"

Zayed gestured to the rumpled bed. "Considering what we have just done? The entire camp knows what has transpired here tonight. Our marriage has been consummated. Most thoroughly.

"Besides, I am a man of honor." And he could not instigate a divorce without first knowing where he stood with Sultan Hassan.

"Are you?" Olivia challenged him shakily. "Because a man of honor would not, it seems to me, abduct a woman and then take her virtue."

Again he felt this guilt, along with a cleaner, stronger anger. "I thought," Zayed bit out, "you were my *bride*."

"And I suppose you think that makes it acceptable? I would say even less so, then."

"I was intending to consummate a marriage that has been planned for nearly twenty years," Zayed snapped. "I admit, taking Princess Halina from her palace bedroom might seem like a drastic action, but I assure you, it was necessary."

"Necessary? Why?"

He didn't really want to go into all the reasons behind the politics, not now, when he was still reeling, his mind spinning, seeking answers when he feared there were none. He was married, and he'd made sure it was done in a way that was legal, binding and permanent. The trouble was, he'd married the wrong woman.

Conveniently Wed!

Conveniently wedded, passionately bedded!

Whether there's a debt to be paid, a will to be obeyed or a business to be saved...she's got no choice but to say, "I do!"

But these billionaire bridegrooms have got another think coming if they imagine marriage will be that easy...

Soon their convenient brides become the objects of an *inconvenient* desire!

Find out what happens after the vows in:

His Merciless Marriage Bargain by Jane Porter

Bought with the Italian's Ring by Tara Pammi

Bound to the Sicilian's Bed by Sharon Kendrick

Imprisoned by the Greek's Ring by Caitlin Crews

Look out for more Conveniently Wed! stories coming soon!

Kate Hewitt

DESERT PRINCE'S
STOLEN BRIDE

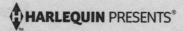

If you purchased this book without a cover you should be aware
that this book is stolen property. It was reported as "unsold and
destroyed" to the publisher, and neither the author nor the
publisher has received any payment for this "stripped book."

Recycling programs
for this product may
not exist in your area.

ISBN-13: 978-1-335-50434-0

Desert Prince's Stolen Bride

First North American publication 2018

Copyright © 2018 by Kate Hewitt

All rights reserved. Except for use in any review, the reproduction or
utilization of this work in whole or in part in any form by any electronic,
mechanical or other means, now known or hereafter invented, including
xerography, photocopying and recording, or in any information storage
or retrieval system, is forbidden without the written permission of the
publisher, Harlequin Enterprises Limited, 22 Adelaide St. West, 40th Floor,
Toronto, Ontario M5H 4E3, Canada.

This is a work of fiction. Names, characters, places and incidents are
either the product of the author's imagination or are used fictitiously,
and any resemblance to actual persons, living or dead, business
establishments, events or locales is entirely coincidental.

This edition published by arrangement with Harlequin Books S.A.

For questions and comments about the quality of this book,
please contact us at CustomerService@Harlequin.com.

® and TM are trademarks of Harlequin Enterprises Limited or its
corporate affiliates. Trademarks indicated with ® are registered in the
United States Patent and Trademark Office, the Canadian Intellectual
Property Office and in other countries.

Printed in U.S.A.

After spending three years as a die-hard New Yorker, **Kate Hewitt** now lives in a small village in the English Lake District with her husband, their five children and a golden retriever. In addition to writing intensely emotional stories, she loves reading, baking and playing chess with her son— she has yet to win against him, but she continues to try. Learn more about Kate at kate-hewitt.com.

Books by Kate Hewitt

Harlequin Presents

The Innocent's One-Night Surrender
Moretti's Marriage Command
Inherited by Ferranti

One Night With Consequences

Engaged for Her Enemy's Heir
Larenzo's Christmas Baby

Seduced by a Sheikh

The Secret Heir of Alazar
The Forced Bride of Alazar

The Billionaire's Legacy

A Di Sione for the Greek's Pleasure

Secret Heirs of Billionaires

Demetriou Demands His Child

The Marakaios Brides

The Marakaios Marriage
The Marakaios Baby

Visit the Author Profile page
at Harlequin.com for more titles.

CHAPTER ONE

HE CAME IN through the window.

Olivia Taylor looked up from the blanket she'd been folding, her mouth dropping open in wordless shock. She was too surprised to be scared. Yet. He was dressed all in black, his body underneath the loose garments tall, lithe and powerful. A turban covered his hair but beneath it Olivia saw his face and the determination blazing in his steel-coloured eyes.

She drew a breath to scream when he moved swiftly towards her and slipped a hand over her mouth. 'I won't hurt you,' he said in Arabic, his tone brusque and yet also strangely gentle. It took her a moment to make out the words; she'd learned some Arabic living in the Amari household, but it was still of the schoolgirl variety. She'd been hired to speak only English to the three youngest Princesses.

He continued speaking and her shocked mind struggled to understand. 'That is my solemn vow, and I will never break it. Just do what I say and no harm shall ever come to you. I swear it on my life.'

Olivia stood there rigidly, his hand on her mouth, the scent of his skin in her nostrils. He smelled of horse and sand and sweat and musk…and, strangely, it was not unpleasing. Her mind was spinning with terrifying numbness, around and around, unable to latch onto any coherent thought. She couldn't think. She could barely breathe. Shock gave way to fear, making her dizzy. It was as if everything were happening underwater or in slow motion, yet far too fast, because already the man was propelling her to the window, and somehow she was going, going, her legs weak as water, her insides sliding around like jelly, her mind a blank canvas of fear and shock.

Halina was in the next room. The door wasn't even closed, not properly. She could hear her friend humming under her breath. How could this be happening? She'd only come in here, to Halina's bedroom, to put away her evening gown and tidy up a bit. Halina had just returned from what she'd claimed was an interminable dinner with her parents to discuss her future. Her fiancé. Olivia knew Halina didn't want to get married, and certainly not to a rebel prince she'd never met.

'He's practically an outlaw,' she'd said as she'd thrown herself on the sofa in her sitting room with a gusty sigh. 'A *criminal*.'

'I heard he went to Cambridge,' Olivia had countered mildly, used to her friend's theatrics, and Halina had rolled her eyes, determined to play up to whatever audience she had.

'He's been living in the desert for ten *years*. He's probably gone completely savage. I don't even know if he speaks English.'

'If he went to Cambridge, I'm sure he speaks English. And in any case your parents don't want you to marry him until his title is fully restored and he's back in the capital, in his palace,' Olivia had reminded her. She'd been governess to Halina's three younger sisters for four years, and she was well versed in all the family's hopes and plans.

Halina had been engaged to Prince Zayed al bin Nur since she was ten years old, but a decade ago his family's rule had been overthrown by a government minister—Fakhir Malouf—and Prince Zayed, only just returned from university, had been forced into exile in the desert to fight for his throne.

Civil war had happened in spurts and bursts over the years, Zayed's band of rebels to Malouf's crack troops. Halina's father had insisted on honouring the betrothal, but only when Zayed's power was fully restored...and who knew when that would be?

But surely this man had nothing to do with that. Why did he want her? Why was he here?

Already he was at the window, one hip braced against the ledge, one hand gripping her upper arm, the other still over her mouth. She could taste the salt on his skin. His breath fanned her ear as he spoke, making her shiver.

'Please, do not be afraid.'

Strangely, she believed him. He didn't want her to be scared—and yet he was *abducting* her. Her frozen brain finally thawing into gear, Olivia started to struggle, her body arching against the man's as she attempted, uselessly, to free herself from his hold.

'Don't do that.' The words were quiet and lethal as his grip tightened on her, his hands like iron bands on her body. Inflexible and impossible to break, yet still strangely gentle. Olivia stilled, her heart thudding, knowing instinctively if she didn't escape now there would not be another good opportunity. And if she didn't escape...

Her mind blurred and blanked. She could not imagine what this man wanted with her, what he intended.

'I said I wouldn't hurt you.' The faintest edge of impatience had entered the man's low, steady voice. 'This is for the best, for both of us.' Which made no sense at all. There was no best for her in being kidnapped. *How* had this man been able to climb in through the window of Halina's bedroom?

The royal palace in the desert kingdom of Abkar was several miles from the capital city, remote and guarded by a high stone wall, patrolled by dogs and soldiers. Hassan Amari took no chances with his precious, beloved family. And yet here was this man, dark, strong, utterly in control. Something had gone very wrong at some point and Olivia couldn't imagine why or how.

The man turned her towards him. His face was very close, his lashes surprisingly long and lush, his eyes not merely grey, as she'd first thought, but a startling, mossy grey-green. His cheeks, nose and mouth were all hewn of harsh lines, giving Olivia an even stronger sense of the grim determination and inflexibility she'd seen in him from the moment he'd come through the window.

'I will keep you safe.' Looping a rope around her waist, he heaved her over the window to plummet down into the desert darkness.

The breath whooshed from Olivia's lungs and she was too startled to scream as the air streamed past, her heart suspended in her chest.

Then the rope jerked taut and she landed with a heavy thud in another man's arms. He righted her quickly, her feet on the ground, but before she could scream he had covered her mouth with a scarf and tied it.

The man who had come in Halina's bedroom was scaling down the side of the palace wall, as stealthy and graceful as a panther. He landed lightly on his feet, his grey-green eyes narrowing at the sight of the gag on Olivia's mouth.

'I'm sorry,' the other man said in a low voice. 'I did not want her to scream.'

The man nodded shortly as Olivia's mind whirled.

What was going on? Why had they taken her?

The man looked back at her, a faint smile curving that rugged mouth. 'Come,' he said and, taking her by the elbow, he drew her towards several horses that were tethered by the palace wall.

Horses? How on earth were they going to get out of the palace on horses? The only way was through the front gates, tall and towering, topped with iron spikes and guarded by Sultan Hassan's private soldiers.

The man heaved her up on a horse and Olivia sprawled inelegantly across its back. She'd never ridden, unlike Halina and her sisters, who had been practically raised on horseback.

The man quirked an eyebrow, seeming almost amused by her ineptitude, and then righted her, swinging up to straddle the horse behind her so she was nestled closely between his hard-packed thighs.

He snaked one arm around her waist to draw her even more tightly against him; Olivia could feel his heart thudding against her back, the heat of his body warming her right through. His scent invaded her senses. She'd never been so close to a man before.

'Let's ride,' the man said in a voice that managed to be both soft and commanding, and they headed off, Olivia watching in disbelief as they rode right through the palace gates, not a soldier in sight. Had these men taken over the palace? Had there been some kind of attack and no one had even realised?

As soon as they were clear, the man took off her gag.

'I am sorry for that. I did not want you to be treated so roughly.'

Which made no sense. He was her *kidnapper*. But Olivia couldn't ask any questions now, not with the wind streaming past and the sand flying into her eyes. The man slowed the horse down to tie the scarf around her hair and cover her mouth. 'There. That is better,' he murmured into her ear, sending shivers racing across her skin.

Olivia was conscious of the hard wall of the man's chest she was leaning against, his arm wrapped so snugly around her she almost felt safe. He kicked his heels into the horse's flanks and they were off again, flying across the sand.

The hours blurred into one another as they kept riding, the man holding her all the while, her body starting to ache from the constant jostling.

The moon was a silver crescent high above them, the sky a garden of stars sending silvery shadows across the desert sand, the only sound the steady thud of the horses' hooves.

At some point Olivia fell into an uneasy doze, her head resting against his chest, which seemed impossible, considering her precarious situation, but the constant, teeth-jarring movement had exhausted her.

She woke with a jolt when their gallop slowed, the man's arm relaxing on her only slightly. Olivia blinked warily; a few flickering lights emerged like pinpricks in the darkness. She heard low, murmuring voices but couldn't make out the words. It had taken concentration to understand everything the man had said to her in Arabic, and Olivia thought she must have missed or misunderstood some words.

The man slowed the horse to a stop and slid off it in one easy movement before turning to her.

Olivia gazed down at him, uncertain and suddenly desperately afraid. They had arrived at some kind of destination, and she had no idea what was going to happen now. What this man was going to do with her. He'd said he wouldn't hurt her, that he would keep her safe, but why on earth should she believe him?

'Come down,' he said quietly, and his tone reminded Olivia of the way Sultan Hassan talked to a frightened mare. 'No one will hurt you. I gave you my vow.'

'Why…?' Her voice came out in a croak; her throat was as dry as dust, sand speckling her lips and skin. 'Why have you taken me?'

'For justice,' the man replied. He reached for her, his hands gripping her arms with that gentle strength she'd felt before. 'Now, come down. Eat, drink, refresh yourself. And then we'll talk.'

Olivia's feet hit the ground and her legs nearly gave way. She hated being so feeble, but she'd never ridden a horse before and they'd been galloping for several hours. Her thighs chafed and her muscles ached. She felt as if she could collapse right where she stood. The man caught her, swearing under his breath.

'I thought you knew how to ride.'

'What?' Olivia blinked at him in surprised

confusion. *Why would he think that?* 'No, I don't know how. I never learned.'

'It seems my intelligence was wrong on one point, at least.' He turned away before she could reply. 'Suma will see to you.'

Zayed al bin Nur strode towards his tent, his body aching from the hard ride and his heart thudding with the heady pulse of triumph. He'd done it. He'd actually done it. He'd successfully kidnapped Princess Halina Amari from behind the seemingly impenetrable walls of the royal palace. All that remained now was to seal the deal and make her his bride.

His mouth curved grimly as he thought of his future father-in-law's fury. Abducting Princess Halina had been a massive risk, but a calculated one. Hassan Amari knew Zayed's cause was just. And Zayed knew he needed the full support of the neighbouring kingdom of Abkar to wage war against Fakhir Malouf, the man who had taken his throne…and murdered his family.

The old rage settled in Zayed's gut, ice-cold and iron-hard with the passage of time, a familiar and almost comforting weight as he ducked under the flap and went into his tent. His advisor and friend, Jahmal, scrambled to attention.

'My Prince.'

'Have the preparations been made?'

'Yes, My Prince.'

Zayed shrugged off his travel-stained cloak and tore the turban from his hair, running his hand through the spiky mass to dislodge the grains of sand. 'Thank you. I am giving my bride half an hour to rest and refresh herself, and then we will go ahead with the ceremony.'

Unease flickered across Jahmal's face but he nodded. 'Yes, My Prince.'

Zayed knew his closest advisors had been deeply unsure about the risk he was taking. They were afraid of invoking Hassan Amari's wrath, even of starting another and far more damaging war with a neighbouring country they counted as their ally. But they didn't have the same fury and fear driving them as he did. They didn't remember the tortured screams of his brother and father as they'd burned to death in a helicopter that had pirouetted to the ground in flames. They didn't see his mother's shocked face when they closed their eyes, feel her unending grief, the memory of her dying in his arms a burden they would carry to his last breath. They didn't wake in the darkness, a silent scream of terror and rage bottled in their throats as the vestiges of a nightmare clung to their shattered minds and they were forced to face another bleak dawn, an unending day of fighting for what always should have been theirs.

No, they didn't understand. And no one ever would. This civil war would go on and on with no end in sight unless Zayed did something drastic and definitive. Fakhir Malouf would continue to set his country back decades, oppressing his people with his hopelessly backward schemes. Zayed *had* to act. And this had been the only option open to him.

There were worse things than a rushed wedding. He was honouring his betrothal vow, that was all. Halina would learn to accept it. Shrugging out of his dusty garments, Zayed prepared to meet his bride.

Half an hour later, freshly bathed and shaven, he ducked into the tent where he had ordered Suma to bring Halina to wait. His eyes adjusting to the flickering candlelight, he saw that she sat on a silken pillow with her back to him, narrow and slender, her hair streaming down it in a dark, damp river. She wore a loose robe of deep blue embroidered with silver thread that engulfed her slender figure but still reminded him of how she'd felt in his arms, slender and light. A surprising surge of desire arrowed through him. This marriage was about politics, nothing more, but it had been a long time since he'd lain with a woman.

Zayed let the tent flap fall closed behind him with a rustle and she turned, scrambling to a standing position, her eyes wide. She had incredible eyes, a deep, stormy blue, fringed extravagantly with sooty lashes. He hadn't expected those eyes, somehow.

Of course, he'd never seen a proper photograph of his bride, merely a few blurry images taken from a distance, since she'd been raised in virtual seclusion. They'd been betrothed when he was twenty and she ten, although it had been done formally, with a proxy, so they'd never met. Now did not seem like the most auspicious of introductions, but there was nothing to be done for it. Zayed squared his shoulders.

'You have been made comfortable, I trust?'

She hesitated, her gaze searching his face, looking for answers. After a pause, she finally answered. 'Yes…' Her voice was both soft and husky, pleasant. That was good. So far he liked her eyes and her hair, and he knew her body was both slender and curvaceous from being nestled against it on horseback for several uncomfortable hours. Three things that he could be thankful for. He had not expected so much. Rumours had painted Halina as a melodramatic and slightly spoiled princess. The woman in front of him did not seem so.

'But…' Her throat worked convulsively, the words coming in stumbling snatches. 'I don't… I don't…understand why you've…'

From behind them the tent flap rustled again and Zayed met the subtly questioning gaze of the imam he'd chosen to perform the ceremony. He would have preferred a civil service, but Malouf would dismiss a marriage that was conducted by a notary, and the last thing he could do was have Malouf dismiss this, the most important diplomatic manoeuvre he'd ever make.

'We're ready,' he said to the imam, who gave a brief nod. Halina's confused gaze moved from him to the man who would marry them.

'What…what are you…?'

'All you need to say is yes,' Zayed informed her shortly. He did not have time for her questions, her concerns, and certainly not her protestations. They could talk after the vows were performed, the marriage finalised. Not before. He would allow nothing to dissuade him. Halina's eyes had widened and darkened to the colour of a storm-tossed sea, her lips, rosy-pink and plump, parting soundlessly.

'Yes,' she repeated, searching his face, looking for answers. Did she not understand what she was doing here? It seemed obvious to Zayed, and it would soon be so to Halina when she made her vows. He could not afford to explain why he'd taken her, why they had to marry with such haste. Although his desert camp was well hidden, already Sultan Hassan could be sending his troops to take back his daughter. Zayed intended to have the marriage performed well before then.

Sensing his urgency, the imam moved forward and began the ceremony, speaking with quick fluidity. Zayed took Halina by her arm, firmly but with gentleness. She looked dazed, but Zayed hoped she'd adjust quickly. She knew they were engaged, after all. His methods might be unorthodox, but the end result would be the same as if they'd been surrounded by pomp and circumstance.

A silence descended in the tent and Zayed realised it was Halina's turn to speak. 'Say yes,' he hissed and she blinked at him, still seeming confused.

'Yes,' she said after a second's pause.

The imam continued twice more, and twice more Zayed had to instruct Halina to speak. *'Say yes.'*

Each time she murmured yes—*naaam*—her lips forming the word hesitantly.

The imam turned to him and Zayed bit out his three replies. Yes, yes, yes.

Then, with a little bow, the imam stepped back. Zayed's breath rushed out in a sigh of satisfaction and relief. It was done. They were wed.

'I'll leave you alone now,' he told Halina, who blinked at him.

'Alone?'

'For a few moments, to ready yourself.' Zayed hesitated, and then decided he would not explain things further. Not now, with the imam listening and Halina seeming so dazed. Later, when they could talk, relax even, he would explain more. There would be food and wine and conversation—a little, at least. Then he would tell her. Tonight was not merely the marriage ceremony but its consummation.

CHAPTER TWO

OLIVIA FELT AS if she'd fallen down a rabbit hole into some awful, alternative reality. She had no idea what was going on; in the tent she'd only understood one word of Arabic out of three, if that. It had seemed as if some official kind of ceremony had been performed, but Olivia had no idea what it could be. And the man had insisted she keep saying yes—but to what? Perhaps he was preparing a ransom demand to the royal family, and wanted her to proclaim she was unharmed.

And she *was* unharmed, but she was also confused and more than a little scared. Who was the man with the terse manner and the gentle eyes? What did he want from her? And what was going to happen next?

The woman who had helped her to bathe and dress earlier, Suma, fetched her from the tent and led her to another, this one luxurious in every detail. Suma handed her some gauzy fabric and Olivia took it uncomprehendingly. Judging by the way Suma mimed her actions, she was meant to change once again. Olivia glanced down at the garment she held, a nightgown of near-diaphanous silk embroidered with gold thread. She had no idea why she had been given such a revealing and exquisite garment but she was afraid to think too much about it.

She couldn't ask Suma; the older woman spoke a dialect of Arabic that was virtually incomprehensible to Olivia. They'd communicated by hand gestures, clumsy miming and the occasional understood word; there was no way she could ask the smiling, round-faced woman what was going on, or why she'd been given this nightgown. Not that Suma would tell her, anyway.

The tent she'd been led to was both sumptuous and spacious, with a mattress on a dais that was spread with hand-woven quilts of silk and satin and scattered with pillows. Candles flickered in torches and the desert wind made the tent rustle quietly. In the distance Olivia could hear the nickering of horses, the occasional low voice.

Suma left her alone to change and Olivia stood there, clutching the nightgown to her, wondering what on earth she was supposed to do now. Escape seemed unwise in the dark; she couldn't ride and they were hours from anywhere. Putting on a slinky, near-transparent nightgown also seemed unwise; the last thing she wanted was to be less dressed.

She put the nightgown on the bed, running her damp palms down the side of the blue robe she'd changed into earlier as she tried to think of a way out of this. Would the man come back? Did he speak English? If he did, perhaps she could demand some answers. Not that he seemed a man to acquiesce to anyone's demands, and Olivia doubted she'd be brave enough to give them.

Suma returned with a platter of fruit and cheese, as well as a jug of something, a carafe of water and two golden goblets. It was all very civilised, Olivia acknowledged with wry incredulity. She was being treated as an honoured guest rather than the prisoner she was...but she still had no idea what her abductor intended to do with her, and thinking too much about it made her stomach churn and bile rise to the back of her throat.

The older woman caught sight of the nightgown Olivia had left on the bed and frowned. She gestured to Olivia to change, and Olivia shook her head.

'No...*la*,' she said, speaking as firmly as she could. Her Arabic was clumsy but insistent. 'I do not want to wear that.'

Suma's frown deepened and she made wild gestures with her hands as she let forth a stream of incomprehensible dictates. Clearly Suma wanted her to wear the gown very much.

'Yes,' Olivia cut across her, having understood at least one word she'd spoken: *jamila*. 'It is very beautiful. But I do not want to wear it.'

Suma scowled. Olivia almost felt apologetic for disappointing her. Was she being reckless, by refusing the nightgown? What if it made the man angry? But why on earth would he want her in it in the first place? A question she could barely bear to ask, much less answer.

With a huff, Suma shook her head and then disappeared. Olivia let out a gusty sigh of relief. She really did not want to parade around a desert camp of strange men in a diaphanous nightgown that looked like something a bride would wear on her wedding night.

She paced the luxurious confines of the tent, wondering if anyone was going to come in to see her and explain what on earth was going on. What did they want from her? If they thought Sultan Hassan would pay a hefty ransom for her return, she suspected they would be disappointed. Hassan was fond enough of her, but she was just an employee.

And if they wanted her for something else…

Swallowing convulsively, she tried not to give

in to panic. She wanted to see the man with the gentle eyes again, although something about his fiercely determined manner made her half hope he wouldn't come in. When he was near her it felt as if he were taking all the air, making it hard to breathe. Hard to think. And Olivia knew she needed all her wits about her now. Somehow she had to figure out why she was here… and then she had to figure out how to escape. Both felt impossible.

Then the tent flap opened and there he was, those grey-green eyes glinting in the candlelight. He was dressed as he had been before, in loose trousers and a long shirt of bleached linen that emphasised the powerful, rippling muscles of his chest and thighs.

Olivia tried not to gulp. She folded her arms and lifted her chin, which was just about all the defiance she had in her. Gazing into that penetrating stare felt like looking at the sun. 'I wish to know why you have taken me here,' she said in English. Surprise flared across the man's face like a ripple in water and then was gone.

'Your English is very good.'

That was because she was half-English. Although as the daughter of a diplomat she'd been raised around the world, her father had been English and that was the language she'd always spoken. 'I prefer English to Arabic.'

'Do you?' His own English was flawless, his tone impossible to decipher. A frown marred his brow for a moment and then smoothed out. 'Why have you not changed?' he asked, with a nod at the nightgown discarded on the bed.

'Why would I want to wear that?' she flung at him. His mouth quirked, impossibly, into a smile. He was actually amused.

'Because it is comfortable? And beautiful. You are, as a point of fact, very beautiful.' He moved past her to a low table flanked by two chairs and the tray with the platter of food on top of it. 'Come, have something to eat and drink.' He gestured to the low folding chair across from him. 'Sit down, be comfortable.'

Olivia could only gape. She was beautiful? No one had ever said that to her before. No one had ever even noticed her before. Why him? Why now? *What did he want?*

He sat down himself, seeming utterly relaxed...and utterly appealing. A tingle went through Olivia just from looking at him. Dark, close-cropped hair, those beautiful eyes the colour of peat, a straight nose and a mobile mouth, the lines and angles of his face both harsh and arresting. As for his body...it was lean and long, every inch of it pure, powerful muscle. Even sprawled in a chair he radiated strength and energy, power and grace.

He was like a jungle cat, ready to spring, eyeing her with a sleepy, knowing, hooded gaze. He could devour her if he wanted. The knowledge flashed through her, certain and strangely thrilling.

She felt a tremor of fear, but with it a pulse of something else. Something almost like desire. He had such a *languid* look in his eyes. No one had ever looked at her like that. She'd spent her life in the shadows, half pretending to be invisible, ignored by her busy, widowed father, and then keeping to the sidelines of school life.

Since becoming the governess to the Amari Princesses four years ago, she'd been even more in the background, which she hadn't minded. That was where she was used to being, making sure she was quietly useful, keeping out of the way of people who were busier or more important than she was. Blending into the background felt both safe and comfortable, and it was only in this heightened, surreal moment she realised how dull it had always been. How dull her whole life had been, as if she had been waiting all along for something to happen. And now it had.

You've been kidnapped, she reminded herself with both fierceness and panic. *This is not some*

*romantic adventure. This man has abducted
you. You need to escape.*

'I want you to release me.'

The man arched an eyebrow. 'Where? Into
the desert?'

'Back to the palace.'

His expression shuttered although he remained relaxed. 'You know that is impossible.'

'How would I know that?'

He made a gesture towards the entrance of
the tent, one Olivia couldn't decipher. What, exactly, was he referring to? 'Too much has happened. Now, come.' He reached for the jug and
poured them both goblets of what looked like
water, but when he added something from another jug the liquid turned milky-white. Olivia
eyed it askance.

'What is that?'

'Arak, mixed with water. It changes colour
when diluted. Surely you have had it before?'

'No.' The only alcohol she had had was the
occasional sip of champagne at Christmas or
New Year when she was a teenager.

'Come, taste it. It is quite refreshing.' He
smiled at her, flashing very white, very straight
teeth. Olivia stayed where she stood. She could
not sit down and have a drink with this man.
He'd *kidnapped* her. 'Well?' He held the glass
out for her, waiting.

'For understandable reasons I am reluctant to take any food or drink from you.'

'Is that so?' Irritation flashed across his face. 'I think the time for such petulant gestures has surely passed?'

Petulant gestures? Olivia bristled even as she recognised a grain of truth in the words. She was hungry and thirsty, and she didn't really think he'd drugged the food. There was no point spiting herself as well as him.

Her chin tilted at a haughty angle that belied the trepidation she felt, she walked over and sat down opposite him. She took the glass he held out, her fingers brushing his and sending another tingle like lightning through her. Her arm jerked in response, everything in her flaring white-hot. The man noticed; Olivia saw it in the brief gleam in his eyes and she felt a rush of embarrassment. She was so innocent, so *gauche*. She could not even hide it. And the fact that she should be attracted to him, her *captor*...

It was both weak and wrong.

'Taste.' His voice was a low, lazy drawl.

Olivia raised the glass to her lips, conscious of the man's gaze resting on her, so languorous and speculative, and she took a cautious sip. 'It tastes like liquorice.'

'It is the anise. Do you like it?'

She took another sip, feeling the fire blaze down her throat and into her belly, warming her right through. 'I... I don't know.'

He laughed softly, the sound winding seductive tendrils around her. She took another sip, craving the courage it provided even as the practical part of her told her drinking more was most unwise. The last thing she wanted to do was let her defences down in front of this stranger, magnetically appealing as he was. He was also dangerous—that Olivia knew for certain, felt all the way to her bones—and getting drunk was definitely not a good idea right now.

'So you have never had arak,' he mused. 'I am pleased to introduce you to a new experience.'

'Are you?' With a slightly unsteady hand Olivia returned the half-drunk glass to the table. She'd only had a few sips and yet already she was feeling the effects of the alcohol, her mind pleasantly blurring at the edges, her body relaxing. That was undoubtedly a bad thing, especially with the way the man was looking at her, with a mix of speculation and, yes, desire. Just as she, impossibly, unwisely, desired him.

A thrill ran through her like an electric shock at the realisation. She was naïve, yes, and completely innocent, but even she could see the heat in his eyes, although she could hardly credit it.

That such a man, a powerful, sensual, attractive man, would want *her*...

But she shouldn't want to be wanted, not by a stranger who was most certainly a threat. Confusion chased desire, leaving her emotions in a ferment. 'Where are we?' she asked, looking away from that heat-filled gaze.

'In the desert.'

'I know that, but where? Are we still in Abkar?'

There was a pause while he cocked his head, his gaze sweeping over her thoroughly, leaving heat and awareness in its wake. He wasn't touching her and yet everything prickled; it was as if parts of her body were stirring to life for the first time. Her breasts, her thighs, her lips. She felt weirdly, achingly conscious of them all, that persistent tingle going right through her, impossible to stop or ignore, obliterating common sense, rational thought.

Disconcerted, Olivia reached for her glass. She'd have just one more sip of the anise-flavoured arak, that was all. She needed a distraction from this unwelcome and overwhelming reaction.

'No, we are not in Abkar,' he said, his gaze still resting on her, considering, assessing. 'We are in Kalidar.'

The country of Halina's fiancé, Prince Zayed

al bin Nur. Was her abduction related to Halina's impending marriage? Was the minister in power, Fakhir Malouf, behind it? Fear trembled in her breast at the prospect and her fingers clenched on the goblet. She had heard terrible things of Malouf, a man who seemed to possess neither mercy nor kindness. This man hardly seemed like a minion of Malouf...but who was he?

The man must have noticed the fear tensing her fingers and flashing in her eyes, for he leaned forward, his gaze blazing silver for one heart-stopping second. 'I have told you, you need never be afraid of me. I know we have had an inauspicious beginning, but you can trust me on that.'

'You kidnapped me from the palace,' Olivia pointed out, glad her voice didn't tremble as her insides did. 'Why shouldn't I be afraid of you? And why on earth should I trust you?'

'Such means were necessary. Unwelcome, I grant you, but very much necessary.'

'Why?'

'Because I had waited long enough and I could wait no longer. But we need not concern ourselves with politics tonight, *hayete*.'

My life. The endearment caught her by surprise, made her feel weirdly exposed, as if the careless words had revealed a need in her she'd been trying to hide. Olivia blinked at him, wishing she hadn't drunk so much of the arak. Her whole body was buzzing, but not just from the alcohol. The effect this man had on her was far more intoxicating than the arak. It hardly seemed possible that she could react so instantly and overwhelmingly to a stranger, and a dangerous one at that, yet…

She could not deny it. He affected her, and he knew it.

With a small smile flirting with his lips, he leaned forward and cut off a wedge of cheese from the platter with a small, wicked-looking knife. He handed the wedge to her, his lids half-lowered, his smile glinting, making Olivia feel another insistent throb of desire, a pulse going through her whole body. 'You should eat something. You have drunk much of the arak, considering you have never tasted it before.'

'I—oh.' Fumbling a bit, Olivia replaced the glass on the table. She would drink no more. After a second's hesitation she took the slice of cheese from him, her fingers brushing his once again, and nibbled it. It was delicious, fresh and tangy, and made her realise how hungry she was. The hours of riding had sapped her strength and given her an appetite.

'Good, yes?'

'Yes, it is very good.'

He cut a wedge for himself and popped it in his mouth. 'Have some grapes,' he said after he had swallowed, and he took a bunch from the table.

Olivia finished her cheese, mesmerised by the sight of his long, lean fingers tearing off a bunch of the grapes. Everything about the man was sensual, *sexual*. She couldn't escape it, couldn't ignore the heat snaking through her, pooling low in her belly, the tension and expectancy shimmering in the air. It was all so unfamiliar yet felt so…wonderful.

There was no other word for it, strange as it seemed. She felt as if she'd imbibed some secret elixir and it now flowed through her veins. She craved even more of it, the fizzing fireworks, the slow, molten uncurling inside her, even as a part of her insisted she stop, she back away, she stay safe.

She reached for the grapes but with a smile the man gave a little shake of his head and plucked one from the bunch, holding it out between his fingers, a sleepy challenge now in that heavy-lidded gaze. Olivia stared at him uncertainly.

'Open your mouth,' he said softly, and her eyes widened with shock. The invitation was so blatant, except it wasn't an invitation at all. It was a command, and one she should most certainly refuse. She should demand he release her; she should be acting outraged and angry, or even just afraid. Anything but this meek and wilful obedience, already enslaved to her own desire, and yearning for his. She was complicit in whatever was happening here, unspooling between them in a golden thread of sensation. Wordlessly, her gaze fixed on his, she opened her mouth.

Triumph and desire flared white-hot through Zayed as Halina parted her lips. She really was the most beguiling creature, seemingly without artifice…and perhaps she truly was. Perhaps he should take her at face value, although heaven knew that was not something he did, ever. He trusted no one, not even those closest to him. He could not afford to. But his bride's innocence seemed total, her wide blue eyes utterly without guile, every reaction refreshingly honest, even a little gauche. She hid nothing. Perhaps he could at least trust that.

Letting his gaze linger on hers, letting her see the heat and need in it, he slid the grape into her mouth, brushing her full lower lip with his thumb. Halina gave a soft little gasp as she jerked back, her lips closing over the grape, her eyes heartbreakingly wide, reflecting every

emotion as sensations chased through her—
the taste of the grape, the touch of his fingers.

'Delicious,' Zayed said, his voice caressing
the syllables, his gaze still on her. Her dark
hair tumbled in silken waves about her shoulders, sooty lashes sweeping down to hide those
stormy eyes. Where her tunic top gaped he
could see the shadowy curves of her breasts
and hips and it made him ache. She was utterly delectable, and he found he couldn't wait
to taste her.

And wait he would not… With every minute
that passed, Zayed knew Sultan Hassan could
be coming closer, sending out soldiers to res-
cue his daughter. Zayed needed their marriage
to be unimpeachable by then. He needed it to
be consummated. And, judging from Halina's
trembling reactions, she was not averse. Shy,
perhaps, and undoubtedly innocent, but most
certainly not averse.

She swallowed the grape with a gulp, lashes
lifting as she gazed at him in obvious confusion. 'Why are you doing this?'

Zayed leaned forward again. 'Because I find
you so very desirable, *hayete*.' The endearment
came naturally—she was his life, the key to all
his ambitions, all his desires. And, while his
body stirred and strained with sexual need, that
was what he had to remember. This marriage

was essential to retrieving his throne. His inheritance. His life.

'But...' Her tongue darted out to moisten those full, lush lips. Zayed nearly groaned at the artless gesture that had lust arrowing through him. 'But you don't even know me.'

'I know enough. And this was always going to happen, *hayete*, was it not? It was decreed long before now. It was written in the stars.' Flowery language for what had been a businesslike betrothal when they had been both so young, but it was a means to an end. His bride's eyes widened and she seemed startled, and then shyly pleased. The words worked.

'Was it?' She shook her head to clear it. 'Was that why you kidnapped me?'

'But of course.' He had taken her out of desire, but of a different kind. 'Come,' Zayed said and, standing, he reached for her hand and drew her towards him, letting his fingers slide along and then twine with hers.

Her whole body trembled as she stood before him, her head lowered, her lashes fanning her cheeks. 'What...?' Her voice was no more than a thread of sound. 'What do you want with me?'

'I want to make love to you.' Zayed rested his hands on her shoulders, felt how impossibly slender she was, how fragile. 'Slowly and sweetly.' He bent his head to brush a kiss against her temple; her skin was soft and cool. 'Is that what you want?' His lips moved lower to press a kiss to the side of her neck. A shudder went through her body.

'I… I don't… I haven't…' In her nervousness she stuttered, and Zayed laughed softly, kissing the nape of her neck, letting his mouth linger. She smelled of lemons.

'*Hayete*, I know.'

'But…but…surely you didn't bring me here for this?' A soft moan escaped her as he placed one hand on her waist, fingers splaying to brush her hip and the underside of her breast. Her reaction to him was so complete and overwhelming it made the need arrow even more strongly inside him.

'What if I did?' he murmured, stroking the side of her breast with knowing fingers. He needed to go slowly, of course, but it was hard. Harder than he'd expected. His body was demanding to be sated, his thirst slaked. And his bride was so very willing in his arms, trembling as she was, her gaze wide and wondering as she tilted her head to gaze up at him.

'You *did…*'

Was she painting some romantic picture of him as a white knight coming to steal her away because he couldn't resist her? The prospect was laughable, yet so what if she believed it? If it helped in the moment, then so be it. He did desire her. Immensely. And that was enough.

'I did,' he assured her, and then he captured her mouth in a kiss.

CHAPTER THREE

IT WAS A kiss that stole her breath as well as a little bit of her soul. It was the first kiss Olivia had ever had, and she swayed beneath it as the man's mouth moved persuasively over hers.

Her body was awash with sensation, her mind dazed and reeling. She'd never expected this to happen. She'd never expected to feel this way. She was being seduced, ruthlessly and thoroughly, and she couldn't even resist. She didn't want to. The pleasure coursing through her in a hot, honeyed river was too strong for that.

The inner protestations that this man was a danger, her enemy, her abductor, fell utterly silent. She no longer cared. Even if this was merely a night and the man, stranger that he was, used her and then tossed her aside afterwards, Olivia knew she could not turn away from this. Not when she'd finally woken up, after a lifetime of sleeping. Not when every sense and nerve was tuned exquisitely, acutely. She *felt*. She felt so many wonderful things.

Tentatively, learning the steps of this new and intricate dance, she reached up to grip his shoulders, her fingertips grazing his skull. She pressed her body against his, thrilling to the feel of his hard, muscled chest and powerful thighs. And more than that...even in her innocence she recognised the insistent throb of his arousal against her stomach. She'd seen enough films, read enough romance novels, to recognise it and she thrilled to it, to him, all the more.

A groan escaped him as he tore his mouth from hers and took a step back from her. His expression was nearly as befuddled as her own, Olivia thought. They were both breathing heavily, staring at each other in dazed desire, the very air between them seeming to shimmer.

'Come to bed,' he said, and reached for her hand.

For a second Olivia hesitated. Here was the moment of clarity, of choice. Was she really willing to give up her virginity to a stranger? Would she do this, the most intimate and sacred of acts, with a man whose name she did not even know, who had kidnapped her, who had to be merely using her, no matter what flowery language he used? And yet he wanted her. That was no lie, no trick. He wanted her…and she loved the feeling of being wanted.

His fingers found hers and he tugged gently, a smile curving that mobile mouth. 'Do not be afraid, *hayete*. Remember when I said I would never hurt you. That is, and always will be, my solemn vow.'

He spoke as if he knew her, as if he had been waiting for this moment. Waiting for her. Olivia knew he couldn't have been. It was just words, sentiment, yet she believed him in this at least: he wouldn't hurt her. She wouldn't let herself get hurt. A night and no more. How many women had made the same bargain, the same promise? There need be no regrets. She didn't care who he was. All that mattered was what he made her feel right now.

He must have sensed her acquiescence for his mouth curved in a deeper smile, and Olivia saw the triumph flare in his eyes along with the desire. He pulled her gently towards him and she came, hips swaying, heart beating. Their bodies nudged and bumped and he gazed down at her, standing so close she could feel the beat of his heart against her own.

'You are very beautiful. Very desirable.'

No one had ever said such things to her before. She was too skinny, too quiet, all hair and eyes. She didn't have Halina's generous curves and lush mouth, her engaging smile and contagious laughter. She always stayed in the background and no one ever noticed her at all. Until now.

Shyly she laid her hand on his chest, felt the steady thud of his heart underneath the press of her palm. 'As are you.'

He laughed softly at that, and then he took her hand and raised it to his mouth, kissing her palm, his gaze never leaving hers. 'Then we are well matched,' he murmured, and his mouth moved from her palm to her fingertips, kissing and nibbling each one in turn until Olivia's knees went weak.

The man drew her to the mattress, bringing her down to its feathery softness, the silken covers slippery beneath her. He stretched out alongside her, his body relaxed but his gaze so intent.

'So very beautiful,' he murmured. 'But I want to see all of you. May I?'

Everything in Olivia trembled. 'Yes,' she whispered, unable to say anything more. He tugged at the ties of her robe so it fell open, revealing the simple chemise she wore underneath. Keeping his gaze on her, he reached out and cupped her breast, his thumb sliding over the peak, making her shudder. She'd never been touched so intimately, so knowingly.

'You like that?' he murmured, and she nodded jerkily.

'Yes.'

He lowered his mouth to where his hand had just touched, and Olivia jerked again, arching off the mattress as his mouth closed over her breast, damp and hot, sending darts of intense sensation through her. She gripped his head, unsure if she wanted to anchor him to her or push him away, because it was so much. All her nerve endings felt flayed, yet she wanted more of him.

He moved his mouth to her other breast and she gasped out loud. The novels and films had never described it like this. And then he was moving lower, placing lazy kisses along her abdomen, her navel, and then lower still.

Olivia tensed as he nudged her thighs apart. Surely not…? But he was, his warm breath fanning her very centre, and she let out a long, shuddering sigh as he kissed her in the most intimate way possible. Pleasure licked through her veins and her hips arched helplessly, her fingers threaded through his hair, her body on fire. She'd never, ever felt anything like it; it *consumed* her. He did.

And then she felt as if she were burning right up; she cried out loud, a jagged sound, as pleasure exploded inside her, took her over, blaz-

ing through her. When she came to, everything
hazy around her, he'd come up to rest on his
forearms and was smiling down at her.

'And that's just the beginning.'

The *beginning*? He'd kill her, at this rate. Kill
her with pleasure. He laughed softly. 'Don't look
so disbelieving, *hayete*. I intend to make this a
night you shall never forget.'

He already had. Still smiling, he shrugged
out of his own clothes and then rid her of the
rest of her own. Their bodies came together,
naked, skin on skin, limbs twining and tan-
gling. It felt so intensely intimate, to be pressed
against someone like that, every part of herself
on display, on offer for him. And he took it, his
gaze roving over her, his mouth curved, his eyes
gleaming with pleasure. He liked what he saw,
and that thrilled her.

'Touch me,' he commanded, his voice a throb,
and she gazed at him in surprise. Then, hesitantly, she let her hands drift from his powerful
shoulders to the satiny skin of his back, and then
down to his hips. His arousal pulsed against
her, exciting and terrifying her all at once. But
he'd told her not to be afraid, and somehow she
wasn't.

'Touch me,' he said again, his voice ragged,
and Olivia knew what he meant. Feeling shy
and bold at the same time, she moved her hand

from his hip to curl around the pulsing length of his arousal. His breath hissed between his teeth as she stroked him, hardly able to believe that she could create this response in a man so fierce and beautiful.

He kissed her again, hard, the lazy sensuality he'd shown earlier now becoming something far more raw and primal that Olivia matched, the heat and need an insistent pulse inside her, an ache that demanded satiation—again.

He slid his fingers to her core, moving against her slick heat, making her moan. 'You're ready,' he said and Olivia tensed, knowing she was, of course she was, and yet…

Slowly, surely, he slid inside her, an invasion that felt both shocking and overwhelming, the smooth slide of him filling her right up. She gasped out loud, her hips twitching in instinctive discomfort as she struggled to accommodate the sheer size of him.

Sweat sheened on his brow as he braced himself on his forearms and held himself still inside her, waiting for her to adjust to the entirely unfamiliar sensation. 'You are not hurt?' he asked through gritted teeth. Holding back was clearly a huge effort.

Wordlessly Olivia shook her head. She felt too overwhelmed to speak, too emotional. The dazed pleasure that had drugged her senses was trickling away, replaced by a tidal wave of realisation at the enormity of what she'd done. What could not be undone.

As if sensing her thoughts, he brushed a tendril of hair from her forehead and then pressed a kiss against her temple, the gesture almost as intimate as the pulse of his body inside hers. 'It is all right, *hayete*. This is right, what is between us. There is no shame in it. None at all.'

Her body was relaxing into him, instinctively learning his shape, accepting it, and his words were the balm she so desperately needed. She put her arms around his taut shoulders, drawing him closer, bringing him even more fully into herself, gasping at the feel of it. It was as if he'd gone right into her centre, invaded her soul.

'Please,' she whispered, needing something more from him, craving it. *'Please.'* And then he began to move, each slow thrust creating a delicious friction that had the pleasure rushing back, lapping at her senses in wave after wave of sensation and then engulfing her entirely.

Her cry shattered the still air as he pulsed inside her and her body felt as if it were dissolving into sated fragments. She cried again, a sob of joy and wonder, as she pressed her face against his damp shoulder, her body shuddering underneath his as the waves subsided but the wonder remained.

* * *

Zayed held his bride in his arms as she shuddered and wept, clearly overwhelmed by what they had experienced. Hell, but he was overwhelmed too. It had been a long time since he'd lain with a woman, a very long time. Yet he didn't think it had ever felt like this.

Was it different, perhaps, knowing his life was linked with this woman for ever? She would bear his children; she would stand by his side. She was his bride, his wife, his Queen. Yet none of that had been in his mind when he'd held her, when he'd been inside her. The need to consume her had been too overpowering—and that was a dangerous thing.

He didn't need people, just as he didn't trust them. Betrayal had taught him the latter; grief had taught him the first. Zayed rolled onto his back and stared up at the roof of the tent as Halina lay quietly beside him, faint tremors still going through her body.

'You are not in any discomfort?' he asked eventually and she pushed her hair away from her flushed face.

'No…no.' She looked rosy and satisfied and a little bit uncertain. He wanted her all over again, so he rolled away from her, into a sitting position.

'Good.' It was done. Nothing could break the

bond they'd created; she was his wife both in name and physical fact. Zayed rose from the mattress in one fluid movement and shrugged on his clothes.

'Where are you going?' Halina asked. She suddenly sounded very young, and Zayed was reminded that she was only twenty-two—ten years younger than him.

'I have things to do.' His voice came out brusque so he tried to moderate it. 'I will see you later.'

'You will?'

'Of course.' He suppressed a flash of annoyance. Already she sounded needy, clinging, and that was the last thing he wanted. 'If you need anything, you can ask Suma.'

'Suma? But I can't understand her.'

The flash of annoyance came again, and with it an odd sense of unease. 'What do you mean?'

'She speaks a dialect I can't understand.' She was clutching a sheet to her breasts, her hair tumbled around her face. Zayed fought the urge to climb back into the bed and take her in his arms all over again.

'I did not realise she was so difficult to understand,' he said stiffly. 'You will have to get used to it. She is the only woman here to serve your needs.'

'But…what…what are you going to do with me?' Her voice was both tremulous and brave.

Zayed's gaze narrowed. 'What am I going to do with you? I have already done it, *hayete*. It is finished.'

She bit her lip. 'I know that. I mean, I wasn't expecting more than…than this. But now what are you going to…? Why did you kidnap me?' She lifted her chin, holding her gaze steady as if steeling herself for a blow.

Zayed stared at her, completely nonplussed. '*Why* did I kidnap you?' he repeated. 'Surely that is obvious? I told you I could not wait any longer.' He blew out a breath. 'Your father will not be pleased, I grant you, but he will not be able to affect the outcome. Of that I am certain.'

Now she looked genuinely confused, her brow creased, her lips parting. 'My father…' She shook her head slowly. 'But my father is dead.'

'*What?*' Zayed stared at her in complete shock. Sultan Hassan *dead*? When? How? But no; surely he would have heard of it? He would have known. His informants in the palace would have said something. Still, a cold fist clutched his heart. If Sultan Hassan was dead, all his plans fell apart, crumbled to dust. To nothing. The man had no sons, and his heir was a distant cousin, someone Zayed could not rely on to help him. 'When did this happen?' he bit out.

His bride stared at him in wary confusion. 'Years ago. Five years now.' She frowned. 'I don't understand. What could my father possibly have to do with any of this?'

'Wait.' Zayed felt as if he'd entered some weird, alternative reality. How could Halina be saying this? Sultan Hassan had most certainly not died five years ago. What the hell was going on?

'Why do you care about my father?' she asked, her voice trembling. 'Who *are* you?'

For a moment he could only stare. She knew who he was. She *had* to know. 'I am Prince Zayed al bin Nur,' he said, biting off each word. She'd wed him, she'd slept with him! Of course she'd known he was her fiancé, her intended husband. Because, if she hadn't known, why the hell had she slept with him? Agreed to marry him?

'Zayed…' Her face had gone pale, her lips bloodless, dawning horror in her eyes. Something was very, very wrong, and the cold fist that was clutching Zayed's heart squeezed painfully.

'And you,' he said forcefully, each word a throb of insistent intensity, 'are Princess Halina Amari.' She had to be. He'd seen photographs—

blurry, yes, but he'd watched her in the palace. She'd played with her sisters; she'd gone into her bedroom. She had to be his intended bride. His wife.

But already she was shaking her head.

'No,' she whispered. 'No, I'm not Halina.'

CHAPTER FOUR

REALISATION UPON REALISATION was crashing through Olivia, filling her with more and more horror. This was Prince Zayed, her friend's fiancé, and she'd *slept* with him. And he'd thought she was Halina! He'd taken her from the palace believing her to be his bride-to-be. Had this been some sort of romantic seduction, and she'd botched it completely?

'If you're not Princess Halina,' Zayed asked through gritted teeth, his eyes narrowed to silvery slits, every muscle tensing as if for a fight, 'then who the hell *are* you?'

Olivia swallowed hard, her heart beating like a wild bird inside her chest. She clutched the blanket to her, more than ever conscious of her nakedness. 'My name is Olivia Taylor. I'm governess to the Amari Princesses.'

He stared at her for a single second and then he swore, viciously and fluently. Olivia flinched, and wondered if his solemn vow not to hurt her still stood. She had a feeling it didn't, although Zayed kept himself restrained, that pulsing fury leashed, if barely.

'Why, then,' he asked, his voice one of tightly controlled and yet clearly explosive anger, 'did you sleep with me?'

'I...' There was no excuse, no explanation. She'd lost her head, her *virginity* to a stranger. And he'd thought he was bedding his future bride! Olivia closed her eyes, wanting to blot out her shame, erase everything that had happened in the last few hours.

And yet, with the flickers of pleasure still pulsing through her body, she couldn't quite make herself regret it. In Zayed's arms she'd felt so cherished; what a joke. He hadn't even realised who she was. The knowledge of how she'd been duped, how she'd let herself be duped and talked herself into bed with a stranger, was utterly shaming.

'I...' she tried again, and then shrugged helplessly. She had no answer, except that she'd been completely swept away by the force of him, of her attraction to him, and she wasn't courageous or stupid enough to admit that. Surely it had been obvious, anyway?

Zayed whirled away from her in one abrupt movement, raking a hand through his hair. 'Didn't you know who I was?'

'No.'

'And yet you slept with me.'

'You slept with me,' Olivia fired back, finding her courage. She wasn't going to take *all* the blame. 'And obviously you didn't know who I was.'

'Obviously.' The single word was scathing. 'But I would have expected you to correct my mistake, preferably before we'd said our vows.'

'Vows?' Olivia stared at him, dread seeping into her stomach like acid. 'What do you mean—'

'Unless,' Zayed cut across her, ruthless now, any gentleness well and truly gone as his face, his body, his voice all hardened. 'You meant this to happen?'

'Meant it to happen?' Olivia stared at him in outrage. 'I meant for you to kidnap me? I planned it? Are you *insane*?' She could hardly believe she was talking to a prince this way— she, meek Olivia Taylor—but the situation was so surreal, his suggestion so ludicrous and insulting, that for a moment she forgot who she was. Where she was. And even what had happened.

Zayed had the grace to look slightly abashed for a millisecond, and then he simply looked impatient. 'No, not then, of course. But after. Perhaps you saw an opportunity and took it.

You wanted to better your situation. You said you were a governess?'

Olivia shook her head. 'I have no idea what you're talking about.' She felt furious and humiliated, and she really wished she were wearing some clothes. 'And I certainly don't see how I've bettered my situation.'

Zayed's mouth twisted in something like a sneer. 'Don't you?'

'No, I really don't. But since I'm not Halina, and you're not kidnapping me for ransom or something like that, perhaps you could see fit to return me to the palace.' She spoke with as much as dignity as she could muster, considering she was naked. And near tears, which thankfully she blinked back. She would not cry in front of this man, even if she'd already wept in his arms. Even if she'd already experienced more vulnerability and pleasure, more heights and depths, than she had with any other person, ever. Just the memory of how he'd felt inside her, how she'd felt in his arms, the completeness of it, made heat scorch through her, along with something more powerful and dangerous, a longing she could not bear to name. 'I would like to go back home,' she added stiffly.

Zayed stared at her unblinkingly for several long, taut moments. 'Clearly,' he said finally, his voice clipped, 'that is impossible at this juncture.'

'Clearly?' Olivia tried for a look of disdain. 'I don't see how that is at all clear.' Holding the blanket to her, she scooted out of bed and grabbed the diaphanous robe she'd refused to wear earlier in the evening. Her more modest robe was on the other side of the bed, where Zayed had tossed it after undressing her only a short while ago—it felt like a lifetime. A terrible lifetime. She shrugged into the robe, tying the sash as tightly as she could. It wasn't much coverage, but at least it was something. She folded her arms over her breasts and lifted her chin, giving Zayed as challenging a stare as she could. 'So why exactly can't you return me to Abkar?'

Zayed's gaze was penetrating, relentless. His mouth had thinned into a hard, unforgiving line, his eyes blazing steel. Anger and animosity rolled off him in thick, choking waves. How on earth had she ever thought he was gentle? 'I don't know what game you are playing,' he said, each precise word feeling like a threat, 'but I advise that you cease immediately. This is no laughing matter, Miss Taylor. Millions of lives are at stake.'

Millions of lives? Surely that was an exaggeration, yet Olivia wasn't about to debate the point. She could see well enough how grim Zayed looked.

'I'm hardly laughing,' she answered levelly. 'You're the one who took me from the palace, Prince Zayed. You're the one who—' Her breath rushed out. *Seduced me.* She couldn't say the words. She'd been so stupidly willing, so *eager*, to be seduced. It beggared belief now, but only moments ago she'd been putty in his arms, wanting only to be moulded to whatever shape he chose. Still she met his gaze. 'I didn't ask for any of this.'

'Not at first, perhaps.' He took a step towards her, a different kind of fire in his eyes, one Olivia recognised, and it made her catch her breath. Even now, he could feel it. She could. The banked heat in his eyes flared to life and she felt its answer scorch through her. 'But later, Olivia,' he said, his voice low and menacing. 'Later you weren't asking. You were *begging*.'

She hated him. Officially, she hated him. Even as she felt the pulse of desire go through her, an insistent throb, she hated him. Damn her treacherous body. She knew Zayed saw it too, from the way his lip curled and his eyes travelled down her body, raking her in one scathing glance. A short while ago he'd made her feel cherished and important, and now he was making her feel tawdry and cheap, more than she ever had before. Everything about this was awful.

'I regret everything that happened between us this evening,' she said stiffly. 'More than you can possibly imagine.'

'You cannot regret it more than I do,' Zayed snapped. He swore again, turning away from her. 'Dear heaven, do you know what this is going to cost? Everything.' His voice choked and for a second he covered his face with his hands. *'Everything.'*

Watching him, Olivia saw a man in torment and she didn't fully understand it. She had a bizarre yet deep-seated urge to comfort him, to make it better. 'Is it because you—you have been unfaithful to Halina? I don't think she expects such fidelity until you're wed. You haven't even met. She'll understand.' She probably wouldn't care. She hadn't wanted to marry Zayed in the first place.

'Unfaithful?' He dropped his hands and let out a bark of humourless laughter. 'I have not merely been *unfaithful.'*

'You mean because you kidnapped me,' she said slowly, as reality caught up with her. 'And Sultan Hassan will know you meant to kidnap his daughter. He might call the engagement off.' He would be angry, she supposed, but that angry? She liked her employer, found him to be generous and carelessly affectionate, but she knew he had a strong and unwavering core of honour and dignity. She had no idea how he'd react to what Zayed had done.

'Might?' Zayed turned around to face her,

his expression one of weary scorn. 'There is no *might*. He most certainly will. He will be furious that I dared to try to take his precious daughter. That I slipped through his defences.'

'How did you? Why were the gates open when we left?'

Zayed shrugged. 'A cousin of a cousin is one of the guards. He has been my spy for years. He made sure the gates were open to me.'

No, Sultan Hassan would not like that. He would be furious that someone had breached his security, and also threatened and maybe even a little scared by how seemingly easily it had been done. Unless...

'They might not even know I'm gone,' Olivia said slowly. She could hardly believe she was trying to help him, this man whom had taken so much from her, whom she had told herself she hated. Perhaps it was simply that ever-present urge she had to be helpful. Needed. Or perhaps it was the connection they shared, whether they wanted to or not. They'd been lovers. It was not something she would forget easily, or ever. 'If no one saw your men come or go...'

'How would they not know you're gone?' Zayed demanded. 'You were in the next room from the Princess. Someone would come looking for you.'

'Not necessarily.' It hurt a little to admit it,

but Olivia ploughed on. 'I'm the governess, Prince Zayed, not one of the Princesses, and it was late. Princess Halina might be annoyed that I didn't say goodnight to her, but she would have assumed I'd gone to bed. No one will miss me till morning.'

Outside the tent silvery-pink light streaked the sky. It was just coming on to dawn and they were several hours' ride from the palace. 'You could return me,' she pressed, surprised and a little alarmed by the weird shaft of disappointment that went through her at that prospect. Surely this was the best solution, what she wanted? What she *had* to want? No other option made sense. 'And no one would be the wiser,' she added.

'And you wouldn't say anything?' He looked disbelieving. 'You wouldn't tell your employer of your kidnapping?'

'I do not wish people to know what has happened as much as you,' Olivia returned. The thought of Halina learning what she'd done with her fiancé… Olivia's stomach swooped. How could she have been so *stupid*? So utterly reckless? She'd never acted like that before in her life. 'Surely you can understand that?' she challenged Zayed, her voice rising a little.

'Yes, of course, but…'

For a second Zayed looked tempted. Torn. To

make this all go away…they both wanted that. Of course they did. But yet again she felt that inexplicable disappointment flickering through her. Zayed shook his head. 'No, it is impossible.'

'Why?' The word burst out of Olivia and that flicker of disappointment faded away. She couldn't turn back the clock, but returning to Abkar was the next best thing, especially if her abduction hadn't yet been remarked upon. In a few hours she could be in her own bed and she could put the memory of this night completely behind her as if it had never happened…even if she knew she would never, ever forget it, or the feel of being in Zayed's arms.

'For many reasons,' Zayed said shortly. 'None of which you seem to have taken into consideration.'

'Then perhaps you could enlighten me,' Olivia snapped as her patience started to fray. She never spoke out like this, but some strange courage seemed to have taken hold of her. 'Instead of treating me like some sort of imbecile.'

Zayed stared at the woman he'd wed—his *bride*—with a mixture of frustration and despair. This was a complete disaster, one he was still reeling from. And yet, reeling as he was, a leaden weight had settled in his stomach, making him realise this could not be undone as easily as Olivia seemed to think. Of course it couldn't.

'Because too many people know. The Sultan's soldiers, my own people, the imam.' Who, at his instruction, would have shared the news throughout Kalidar that he had wedded and bedded Princess Halina. He had wanted the news to spread to strengthen his claim. He had never envisioned something like this happening.

'The imam?' She stared at him, stormy eyes narrowing. 'What imam?'

Impatience bit at him, chasing the fury and fear. 'The man who married us, of course.'

Olivia's mouth dropped open in wordless shock. '*Married?* But…'

Zayed stared at her, yet another unwelcome realisation flashing through him. 'You didn't know.' It was a statement, and one that was confirmed by the emphatic shake of her head. 'You don't speak Arabic,' he stated flatly. No wonder she had seemed so confused during their rushed wedding. He'd assumed she'd just been overwhelmed by events, but she hadn't actually known what was going on. Known that he'd been hurrying her into a binding, lifelong commitment.

For the first time he felt a flash of true shame for the way he'd treated her. His instinct was to blame her for not having revealed her true identity, and it was one he couldn't let go of easily.

He still suspected her motives, her ambition. Why hadn't she said anything all evening long? That part still didn't make sense.

But he'd never actually said who he was. He'd simply assumed she knew. Just as he'd assumed she'd realised they were marrying. *'Say yes,'* he'd told her, impatient to have the thing done. And so she had. An uncomfortable and unwelcome sensation of guilt trumped his suspicions for the moment.

Olivia dropped onto the bed, her robe flying out, revealing tempting glimpses of golden skin. Zayed looked away. Now was not the time for desire. 'How?' she whispered. 'How can we be married?'

'Easily. You said the vows, as did I.'

'I said yes…'

'Exactly.'

'But if I didn't know what I was doing, if I didn't *realise*, surely it can be annulled?'

Zayed gestured to the rumpled bed. 'Considering what we have just done? The entire camp knows what has transpired here tonight. Our marriage has been consummated. Most thoroughly.'

Olivia's cheeks went pink and she looked away. Zayed felt a stab of pity for her. He'd taken her innocence. She'd given it willingly enough, but still. It was a hard burden for a woman to bear, especially in this culture. And, he realised, she was not acting as if she expected to benefit from it. Surely she should be insisting he honour his vows rather than suggesting he seek an annulment? Unless she was playing a long game.

'Are you promised to someone else?' he asked, and she looked up in surprise.

'Promised?' She let out a short laugh. 'No. There's no one like that. There never has been. Obviously.' She looked away. 'You could set me aside, of course,' she said in a low voice. 'A divorce. It's done often enough by men of power.'

And would bring her even more shame. Zayed shook his head. 'I am a man of honour.' Besides, he could not instigate a divorce without first knowing where he stood with Sultan Hassan.

'Are you?' Olivia challenged him shakily. 'Because a man of honour would not, it seems to me, abduct a woman and then take her virtue.'

Again he felt this guilt, along with a cleaner, stronger anger. 'I thought,' Zayed bit out, 'you were my *bride*.'

'And I suppose you think that makes it acceptable? I would say even less so, then.'

'I was intending to consummate a marriage that has been planned for nearly twenty years,' Zayed snapped. 'I admit, taking Princess Halina from her palace bedroom might seem like a drastic action, but I assure you, it was necessary.'

'Necessary? Why?'

He didn't really want to go into all the reasons behind the politics, not now when he was still reeling, his mind spinning, seeking answers when he feared there were none. He was married, and he'd made sure it was done in a way that was legal, binding and permanent. The trouble was, he'd married the wrong woman.

How could he have been so stupid? So rash? The events of the evening blurred in his mind; he'd been fuelled by both determination and desperation, needing to get it done, and quickly. So he had.

In one abrupt movement Zayed strode to the table and poured himself a healthy measure of arak. From behind him Olivia laughed softly.

'That's what got us into this trouble in the first place.'

'What do you mean?' He tossed it down in one burning swallow and then turned around. 'Are you saying you wouldn't have slept with me if you hadn't been drunk?' Another reason to be appalled by his own behaviour.

'I wasn't drunk.' Olivia glanced down. 'But my inhibitions were loosened, I suppose.'

Zayed thought of the way she'd arched and writhed beneath him, drawing him into her body, begging him to continue. Yes, they certainly had been loosened. And so had his. For a little while he'd lost sight of himself, and all he needed to achieve, when he'd been in Olivia's arms. When he'd felt the sweet purity of her response. It had pierced him like an arrow, it had shattered his defences, but thankfully he'd been quick to build them back up again.

And now he needed to think. He poured himself another measure of arak and sat down to drink it slowly, his mind starting to click into gear. 'Why were you in Princess Halina's bedroom, as a matter of interest?'

Olivia looked at him warily, as if suspecting a trap. Perhaps there was one. He had to know if she was hiding something. Had she known of the plot—had she positioned herself to be taken? Perhaps she'd been acting on Halina's behalf; Zayed had heard that his bride was less than enthused about their nuptials. Or maybe Olivia had seen a chance to better her seemingly small prospects and become Queen. The truth was, he knew nothing about her, and he had every reason to suspect her motives and actions. What gently reared woman fell into bed with a stranger without even asking his name or telling her her own? And not a just a stranger but a man who had kidnapped her, for heaven's sake. Olivia's actions bordered on incredible in the truest sense of the word.

'I was putting her clothes away,' she said after a pause.

'You said you were a governess, not a maid.'

Olivia shrugged, her robe sliding off her shoulder. 'Lina and I were friends in school. That's how I got the position. I was in her sitting room, talking with her after she'd returned from dinner, and tidying up as I did it. Nothing unusual, really.'

'Where was Halina?'

'Sitting on the sofa. She was in the next room when you came in through the window. I could hear her humming.' Olivia shook her head slowly, her eyes wide. 'This all feels so completely surreal.'

And yet, unfortunately for both of them, it wasn't. He hadn't even seen Halina. In truth, he'd only had eyes for Olivia. Even through the blur of binoculars he'd been arrested by her slender form, her movements of efficient grace. And yet...

'You look like her.'

Olivia frowned. 'You think I look like her? No.' She shook her head. 'Not really. A pale shadow, perhaps.'

A pale shadow? It was a revealing choice of words. 'You have the same colouring,' he continued. 'Dark hair...'

'Halina is much prettier than I am,' Olivia

insisted. 'Her hair is darker and wavier and...'
She paused, biting her lip, and Zayed raised his
eyebrows, curious now.

'And?'

'Her figure is...curvier.' Olivia flushed. 'Everyone thinks she is very beautiful.' The implication seemed to be that they thought Olivia was
not. Yet Zayed had enjoyed her curves, slight as
they were, and her hair—a deep, rich brown—
was dark enough for him. Although, now that
he was studying her properly, not blinded by
the wilful determination he'd felt earlier, he
saw that Olivia was right. She resembled Halina only to a small degree. Her colouring was
lighter, more European, and she was a bit taller
as well as slenderer. Even he could see that, having only glimpsed Halina in blurry photos. So
why hadn't he realised it earlier? Because he'd
been too focused. Too desperate.

'You don't speak Arabic,' he recalled slowly.
'And your name sounds English. Where were
you raised?'

'All over the world. My father was British, a
diplomat. We moved every few years to a new
posting and then I went to boarding school with
Halina in England. My mother was Spanish.'

Was. 'You are an orphan?'

Olivia nodded. 'My mother died when I was
small, my father five years ago when I was sev-

enteen. Since I was a friend of Halina's, Sultan Hassan took me under his protection. It was very kind of him.' Zayed nodded slowly. Hassan had presumably taken Olivia on as a paid employee. It wasn't quite the same, yet Olivia seemed grateful.

He took a sip of arak, needing his senses blunted even if he knew he couldn't afford the luxury. His mind moved in circles, seeking a way out of this trap he'd unwittingly made for himself, but all he felt was it tightening inexorably.

'So people know we're married,' Olivia said slowly. 'Too many people, it seems. What...what will this mean for you? And for Kalidar?'

'I don't know.' He glanced at her from beneath his lashes, suspicious all over again. She seemed too good to be true—innocent and helpful and eager to please, caring more for his situation than her own. *Was* she hoping to become the next Queen of Kalidar? Not that he could offer her that much yet. He had tents in the desert and a small cadre of loyal men. In ten years he had not left the barren desert of his country; he had not wanted to give Malouf an opportunity to seize even more power or let his men think he'd abandoned them. If Olivia was hoping for a life of luxury and ease, it would be a long time coming...but it would come. Was she banking on that? Or had she sacrificed herself for Halina's sake?

What *did* she want?

'I'm sorry,' Olivia said after a moment, her voice soft and sad, and Zayed let out a harsh huff of laughter. Now he really was suspicious. She was laying it on a bit thick, her concern for him and his country, when he'd taken her innocence and ruined her reputation.

'*You're* sorry?'

She hunched one slender shoulder. 'You have more to lose than I do. That's what you meant by "millions," isn't it? The people of Kalidar. This marriage—marriage to Halina—was important to you politically. Wasn't it?' She searched his face, her expression both guileless and compassionate. 'I don't know the details, of course.'

'You don't need to know them.'

'But what will you do if you cannot marry Halina?' Olivia's eyes were round, her hair tousled, her lips parted. Even now she looked desirable, and Zayed wanted her all over again.

He suppressed that painful stab of inconvenient desire. Was this her ploy, to get him to admit that he had to stay married to her? Because he wouldn't do it. He'd make her no promises. He'd made far too many already. 'I don't know what I will do,' Zayed said shortly. 'I have to think.' He looked away, a muscle working in his throat, a pain lodging in his chest like a cold, hard stone. This marriage had been essential. Without it...*without it*...

He *had* to get out of this marriage. He had to make it right with Sultan Hassan. Anything else would be failure, *doom* for his kingship, his country. Far too much was at stake for him to worry about the finer feelings of one forgettable woman.

Zayed rose from his seat while Olivia watched with wide eyes, apprehension visible in every taut line of her body. 'Where are you going?'

'Out,' Zayed said brusquely. 'I need to think.'

'But what...what am I meant to do?'

He raked her with one deliberately dismissive glance, determined not to care about this woman to even the smallest degree. He still suspected her. How could he not? To have fallen into bed with him... Maybe he was being judgemental, but he had to be. Too much was at stake for him to trust her an inch.

'You can do what you like,' he informed her. 'Get some sleep, stay in the tent or wander around. I wouldn't go far, though. Outside this camp there is nothing but barren desert for a hundred miles in any direction. You wouldn't last long, Miss Taylor.'

And, with that parting warning, he stalked out of the tent.

CHAPTER FIVE

OLIVIA CURLED UP on the bed, hugging her knees to her chest. She couldn't even begin to comprehend everything that had happened and, far worse, what it might mean. Married. *Married*.

She'd been an idiot for not realising, or at least not suspecting, something of what had been going on. It had been some kind of ceremony, she could see that now, and through her dazed confusion she'd managed to grasp snatches of words: *commitment...responsibility...vow*. She'd heard it, but she hadn't put it all together to realise what was actually happening. How could she have? She hadn't known her captor was Prince Zayed, or that he thought she was Princess Halina.

But even that was the pinnacle of stupidity, Olivia thought wretchedly. Why would a stranger kidnap her, the governess, a mere servant? Of course he'd thought she was someone else. Someone important.

And as for what had come afterward...as magical as it had been, she couldn't think about that. Couldn't wrap her mind around it...or what it might mean.

Through the tent flap Olivia could see a sliver of dawn sky, a pearly pink lighting up the world. Her body ached with fatigue, and her mind too. She needed to sleep, like Zayed had suggested. And after that... Olivia couldn't even begin to think what the future held.

She stretched out on the bed, inhaling the already familiar musk of Zayed. The feather mattress still bore the indent of their entwined bodies. She closed her eyes, willing herself to sleep. Her mind seethed with remembered sensations, and she felt herself tensing up despite her best efforts to relax. She was never going to get to sleep, yet she knew she needed the rest. Desperately.

Somehow, despite the tumbled thoughts in her mind, the tension in her body, she fell into a restless doze that at some point turned into a deep, dreamless slumber. When she awoke, for a few seconds she couldn't remember what had happened, and she lay there, blinking up at the tent ceiling, her mind fuzzy and blank. Then it came back with a sickening rush, and she closed her eyes as her mind relentlessly played a montage of memories from the night before:

the moment Zayed had come through the window, dark and fearsome, yet with those gentle eyes; then the dizzying fall from the window; the endless hours on horseback…and then…

Olivia let out a rush of breath. Even now she could feel Zayed's mouth on hers, moving so persuasively, his hands caressing her, knowing exactly how to touch her and make her respond. And her own utter wantonness… She hadn't even questioned herself, not really. She'd simply wanted…and taken. Or, rather, let herself be taken.

It had to be mid-morning now; the tent was baking hot, bright sunlight filtering through the entrance flap. The skimpy robe Olivia had put on last night now stuck to her body. She rolled into a sitting position, groaning as her head spun, no doubt from the alcohol she wasn't used to, as well as being dehydrated. From outside the tent she could hear the sounds of activity: men talking in shouts and laughter; a horse nickering. What, she wondered as she held her head in her hands, happened now?

A few moments later Suma came in with a tray of food and drink. She smiled at Olivia, looking pleased.

'You wear the robe,' she said in more distinct Arabic. Zayed must have told her that Olivia had trouble understanding. What else had he said?

How many people knew what had transpired in this tent? Olivia had a feeling it was just about everyone in the camp, and she blushed with the shame of it.

'Yes, thank you,' she answered in her own halting Arabic. Suma put the tray down on the table.

'Come and eat,' she instructed. 'Drink.'

'Thank you.' Olivia realised she was both thirsty and hungry. She'd had little to eat and drink last night besides the arak, a few grapes and a bit of cheese. Remembering how Zayed had fed her a grape made her blush all over again. How could she have allowed him such liberties? Why hadn't she been thinking more sensibly?

'It was a good night,' Suma said with satisfaction. She beamed at Olivia as Olivia sat down at the table and began to serve herself some of the traditional Arabic dishes. There was labneh yogurt with lemon juice, fava beans with mint and fresh cucumber, as well as dates flavoured with cardamom. It all looked delicious. There was also a little brass carafe of coffee that smelled wonderful.

'A bride needs to eat,' Suma added, smiling widely. She looked homely and happy, and even through her embarrassment Olivia's heart went out to her. Did Suma not realise she wasn't the

Princess? That this marriage was a complete disaster? 'Especially if there is a *nunu*.'

For a second Olivia didn't know what she meant; the phrase was colloquial and beyond her understanding. Then she saw Suma pat her stomach meaningfully and realisation rushed through Olivia. A baby. *Especially if there was a baby.* If Zayed had got her pregnant.

She stared at Suma in ill-disguised horror, but the older woman merely took it as maidenly surprise and chortled happily before leaving the tent. Olivia stared down at the plate piled high with various dishes, her mouth dry, her appetite vanished. What if she was pregnant?

It was perfectly possible, she realised with a sick feeling. Her cycle was regular and she was right in the middle of it. Even she in her virginal—or not—innocence knew that this was a peak time for fertility. She could very well be pregnant with Prince Zayed's baby.

Recrimination tore through her, worse than before. She felt like screaming, stomping her feet or, worse, sobbing. How could she have been such a besotted fool? Twenty-two years of living quietly, staying safe, and she'd risked it all in a single night with a stranger. It was as if, last night, she'd become someone else entirely.

The trouble was, she couldn't stay as that person. She wasn't that person. And now she was back to being plain Olivia Taylor, except she was married to a prince and she very well might be expecting his child. She would have laughed at the sheer lunacy of it, if there hadn't been a lump the size of a golf ball in her throat.

Somehow she managed to choke down some of the breakfast. She needed to eat and drink, *nunu* or not. She'd half finished her plate when Suma returned with fresh clothes, thankfully modest. Olivia took the loose tunic and trousers with murmured thanks.

'You wish to wash?' Suma asked, miming washing. 'The oasis has a private area. You go?'

Olivia nodded. She'd like to see something other than this tent, even if she inwardly quailed at the thought of facing a camp full of strangers. With some miming and basic directions, Suma instructed her how to get to a private inlet of the oasis.

Smiling and murmuring her thanks, Olivia took a deep breath and then ducked out of the tent.

'My Prince?'

Zayed started from his ill-humoured reverie to see Jahmal at the entrance to his private tent, a respectful but inquisitive look on his face. Did he know of his mistake? From the guarded curiosity on his aide's face, Zayed doubted it, but Jahmal could sense something was wrong.

'It…went well?' he asked cautiously.

Zayed almost laughed, except there was nothing remotely funny about this situation. Nothing at all. He'd spent the last hour pacing his tent and trying to figure a way out of this mess of his own making. Because it was of his own making, no matter what Olivia Taylor was in it for. If he'd kidnapped the right woman, he would not be here, cursing his fate as well as his own idiocy.

'It went,' he said tersely. He scrubbed his face with his hands, exhaustion crashing through him. He hadn't slept for over twenty-four hours and he didn't foresee much sleep in his future. He still had no idea what to do to fix this situation. Send an envoy to Hassan? How the hell could he explain?

'The Princess is…happy?' Jahmal ventured, his forehead creasing as his dark eyes searched Zayed's fierce expression.

This time Zayed did laugh, because what else could he do? There were no walls to punch, no way to let out the fury he felt, directed solely at himself. For ten years failure had not been an option—and yet after all the war, all the bloodshed, all the loss, grief and pain, he wondered if the last decade had been nothing but failure. And now this.

'I have no idea how the Princess feels,' he told Jahmal, 'because she's not here.'

Jahmal's frown deepened. 'My Prince? I don't understand…'

'I took the wrong woman,' Zayed explained, biting each word off and spitting it out. It was like some ridiculous farce. 'I kidnapped the governess, not Princess Halina.' Colour surged into his face just from stating it so baldly. How could he have been so stupid?

'The wrong woman…' Jahmal's face drained of colour. 'But…did she not say…?'

'No, she didn't say. She didn't protest at the wedding, either.' An hour of sitting here stewing had made suspicion solidify in Zayed. He might be to blame for taking the wrong woman, but why the hell hadn't Olivia spoken up? There had been plenty of opportunity. Why hadn't she asked who he was? He'd assumed she'd known, because she'd never said otherwise. Really, she'd been remarkably quiet, all things considered. And that made him wonder if she'd seen a good deal and decided to take it.

There was, he knew, only one way to find out. Not that it would make much difference to the outcome, but at least it would ease his conscience when he informed Olivia in no uncertain terms that he was divorcing her and

marrying Halina at the earliest opportunity...
and that she would help him to achieve that goal.

After Jahmal left, Zayed decided to go talk
to Olivia. The sooner he could implement some
damage control, the better. But when he went
to the tent, it was empty, and Suma informed
him that Olivia had gone down to the oasis to
bathe. Fine. He would see her there.

The small camp was built around a verdant
oasis, shaped like a kidney, so there were several private inlets. Olivia had gone to one of
these, well out of sight of the camp, and Zayed
strode down the palm-fringed path to the private cove to find her.

He paused as he crested a gently rolling dune;
Olivia was hip-deep in water and wearing absolutely nothing. The breath rushed out of Zayed's lungs as he took in her perfect slender
form, the bright morning sunlight gilding her
body in gold.

She held a cloth above her head, squeezing
it so water dripped out, the droplets running
down her shoulders and back. Desire surged
through him, an irrepressible force. Zayed
clenched his fists, willing it back. Lust for this
woman had weakened him once. It would not
do so again.

He came down the hill, the long grasses that
fringed the oasis rustling as he moved, and Ol-

ivia turned, gasping as she caught sight of him. She rushed to cover herself and Zayed's mouth twisted sardonically. Her maidenly outrage was just a little too melodramatic to be convincing, especially considering what they'd been doing together mere hours ago.

'You don't need to rush,' he drawled as she waded out of the water and snatched a towel. 'I've seen it all before.'

'That doesn't mean you need to see it again.' She knotted the towel above her breasts, her hands shaking. Zayed folded his arms and surveyed her dispassionately. Never mind that she looked utterly lovely, with her dark, damp hair already starting to dry and curl in tendrils about her heart-shaped face. Never mind that her eyes looked huge and blue, and that those thick, sooty lashes drove him to distraction. *Never mind.*

'As soon as possible, I am going to send an envoy to Sultan Hassan, explaining the situation.'

Her eyes widened and Zayed thought he saw disappointment flicker in their stormy depths, vindicating his suspicions. She was in it for herself. She had to be.

'Everything about our situation?' she asked cautiously.

'Word will already have got out.'

'Even so...'

'I am not a liar.' His voice came out hard. 'I will be honest with Hassan, and so will you.'

'Me?'

'You will write him a letter that I will include as part of my correspondence, explaining what happened and how you did not correct my misinformation.'

Anger flared in her eyes and she hugged her arms to herself, hitching the towel higher. 'Correct your misinformation?' she repeated with a surprising edge of acid to her voice. 'I didn't realise it was my responsibility to make sure my abductor's kidnapping attempt went smoothly.' She planted her hands on her hips, making the towel slip and affording Zayed a tantalising glimpse of the rounded curves of her breasts. 'When should I have done that, Prince Zayed? When I was being thrown out of a window? Or when I was gagged on horseback?'

'I removed the gag.' Pain flickered at his temples as he set his jaw.

'Or when I was thrust into a tent and a marriage ceremony without having exchanged a word with you? What should I have done? Said, *Pardon me, but I think you might have the wrong woman*?'

'Surely,' Zayed gritted, 'you realised a mere employee would not be kidnapped?'

'A mere employee.' Hurt flashed in her eyes

and she looked away. Zayed suppressed an un-necessary flicker of guilt. He'd only been stating the truth. It wasn't meant to be an insult. 'I'm afraid I was too overwhelmed and fearful for my life to consider the practicality of it all,' she said after a moment, her gaze still averted.

Rage billowed inside him, rage he knew shouldn't be directed at her, or at least solely at her. Yet he could not keep himself from it. 'And later? When we were in the tent alone, eating and drinking—surely you could have said something then?'

Colour washed over her cheekbones. 'What should I have said?' she asked in a suffocated voice.

'You could have said who you were! You could have asked who I was. We could have avoided consummating the marriage, which would have made things much simpler now.' Olivia didn't answer and Zayed took another step towards her. 'Unless you had no intention of revealing who you were. Or that you knew who I was.' It wasn't quite a question and her gaze swung back to him, her fine eyebrows drawn together.

'What are you implying?'

'That you took advantage of the situation,' Zayed said evenly, ignoring the flicker of unease that rippled through him. Olivia had gone very still, her blue eyes wide, her expression strangely fathomless.

'Advantage,' she said after a moment, her tone as fathomless as her face.

'Yes, advantage. As a lowly governess, essentially a servant in the royal household with few prospects, you saw the advantage in being my wife. Being Queen.'

'Queen? Of what?' Contempt rolled off every syllable. 'A huddle of tents in the desert?'

Zayed flinched under the words, although he knew they were more or less true. 'I will regain my inheritance,' he said in a near growl. 'I promise you that.'

'When? And why would I take such an enormous risk?' She hitched the towel higher, her face flushed now, her eyes bright with anger and even hurt. 'You are contemptible to suggest such a thing.'

'What am I supposed to think?' Zayed demanded. 'There were any number of opportunities for you to tell me who you were.'

'I didn't realise I needed to! Why should I?'

'And what about after?' Zayed took another step towards her; he could smell the freshness of her damp skin, almost feel her quiver. 'What about the wedding night?'

She set her jaw, although her hands shook on the towel. 'What about it?'

'You fell into my arms easily enough. Too easily, I think.'

'It is to my own shame and regret that I did.' Tears trembled on her lashes and she blinked them back. 'Whatever you believe.'

'What woman falls into bed with her kidnapper, without even knowing his name?'

'What man seduces a woman without checking who she is first?' Olivia snapped. 'I accept I was seduced, and far too easily at that. But you are the one who kidnapped me, Prince Zayed. You are the one who took me from my home and forced—'

'I did not force.' The words were low and deadly.

'Not…not that. But the wedding ceremony. You didn't even explain—'

'I thought you knew.'

'Then you made a lot of assumptions, and now you are paying the price, as am I.' With her chin held high, Olivia went to move past him, but Zayed grabbed her wrist, feeling the fragile bones beneath her skin.

'We are not done here.'

She whirled around to face him, fury tautening her features, the towel slipping so her breasts spilled out, golden and perfect. Despite everything, or perhaps because of it, desire arrowed through Zayed, impossible to resist. He drew her towards him and she came, willingly, her lips parting, her features already softening. It was that easy. Her instant acquiescence hardened something inside him and he dropped her wrist.

'Even now you are willing,' he said, not bothering to hide his disgust, and Olivia flushed crimson as she yanked the towel back up.

'As were you,' she choked. 'Don't deny it.'

'I am not now,' he told her coldly, and then turned away, only to still when he saw Jahmal coming over the hill. How much had his aide seen?

'My Prince.' Jahmal's gaze flicked to Olivia and then away again quickly. 'Forgive my interruption, but a message has just come through.'

'A message?' Zayed tensed, wondering if Hassan had already heard, was already angry. If he broke the betrothal... Except, of course, Zayed had already broken it by marrying another woman.

'It is Malouf.'

Olivia might not have understood the Arabic, but she clearly understood that name, for she gasped softly.

'What has he done?' Zayed demanded.

'He sent some men to raid a village two hours' ride from here. There are wounded.'

Zayed swore. Malouf wreaked his bloody war to no purpose and innocents paid the price.

'Let us depart at once.' He started to stride from the oasis when Olivia's voice stopped him.

'Wait!' she cried, and Zayed turned around impatiently.

'What is it?'

She stretched out one slender hand. 'Take me with you.'

CHAPTER SIX

OLIVIA WATCHED AS Zayed's eyes flared with both impatience and irritation and knew he would consider no such thing. She was a liability, a burden, in every possible way. He despised her, it seemed, for having given in to him...just as she despised herself.

And yet she didn't want to be abandoned. Who knew when Zayed would come back? He might leave her here to languish; conveniently forget about her while he pursed his political destiny. And, more importantly, she wanted to do something, to feel useful, rather than sit and wait and worry. If she went with Zayed, she could help.

'Take me with you,' she said again, her voice stronger now. 'I have training in first aid, and I can help if any women or children have been hurt.' She pulled the towel around her more tightly, conscious of the other man's carefully averted gaze. 'I can be of use; I know it.'

Zayed's lips thinned and his eyes narrowed. 'But you don't speak Arabic.'

'I speak enough.' Olivia lifted her chin, willing him to agree. She was afraid to be left here, alone with strangers. Zayed might hate her at the moment, but at least he knew her. He knew her all too well.

Zayed glanced at the other man, who was keeping a deliberately neutral expression. Then he gave a terse nod. 'Very well. Suma will see you have the appropriate clothes. Jahmal will fetch you in five minutes.'

He strode away from the oasis, followed by Jahmal, and Olivia's breath came out in a whoosh of both relief and trepidation. What had she just got herself into? Yet anything was better than staying here and waiting, wondering. The future seemed like so much fog, impossible to know...and yet terrifying at the same time.

Back at the tent Suma brought her some more clothes—desert boots and a headscarf to keep out the sand. Olivia finished dressing quickly, her fingers shaking as she did up the laces on her boots.

Zayed's horrid accusation ricocheted through her brain, filling her with both shame and fury. How could he think she'd somehow planned this? But what was he supposed to think, when she'd fallen into bed with him so willingly, so instantly? Olivia didn't know what was worse—

Zayed thinking she was a scheming gold-digger or a wanton woman.

Exactly five minutes later Jahmal entered the tent and Olivia followed him out, her heart thudding in her chest.

Prince Zayed was waiting in front of a desert camouflage Jeep parked outside the camp, looking both fierce and royal in combat boots, loose trousers and a camouflage shirt that clung to the muscles of his chest and arms. His agate gaze swept over her, giving nothing away. With one brief nod he indicated she should get into the back of the Jeep, so Olivia did. Zayed climbed into the driver's seat and Jahmal slid in next to him.

The sky was a hard, bright blue, the unforgiving sunlight illuminating the barren desert landscape Olivia had been unable to see last night. She'd glimpsed a bit of it on the way to the oasis but now, as the Jeep started away from the camp, she grasped something of the utter isolation of their location.

Undulating sand dunes swept to the horizon, interspersed with large, jagged-looking boulders. She felt as if they were a million miles from anywhere.

The Jeep jostled over the sand and Olivia leaned back, fatigue crashing over her now that the initial adrenalin burst of her confrontation with Zayed had gone.

What was he going to do with her? He'd mentioned sending an envoy to the palace and her writing a letter. But what on earth could she write? Would Sultan Hassan even employ her after hearing that she'd slept with his daughter's fiancé? The thought of being out of a job, potentially without a reference, filled her with fear.

Even worse was the prospect of being without a home, which filled her with a worse grief. For years she'd called the palace on the outskirts of Abkar's capital city home. She'd loved Sultan Hassan's little daughters, had played with them and plaited their hair, taught them English and teased them about their future husbands. She'd felt part of a family for the first time in her life, even if it had been in a small way, as an employee. She would lose it all, she feared, when Hassan heard about what she'd done. Never mind that Zayed had abducted her; Olivia knew how these things played out in this culture. A woman would not be forgiven.

And now, in the hard, bright light of day, she wondered yet again how she had succumbed so easily. He'd been a stranger, a threat, yet when he'd touched her she hadn't cared. She'd only wanted to feel more, to experience the wonder of desiring and being desired. It was as if her common sense, usually in such abundance, had abandoned her completely. She supposed she wasn't the first woman to be in such a position, but it still smote her sorely.

Still, Zayed would annul the marriage on some obscure grounds, or else simply divorce her. They wouldn't stay married and she would hopefully be able to find another position. The thought made her feel mixed up inside, a jumble of emotions she couldn't let herself untangle quite yet.

She'd felt too much already, from the electric tingle of Zayed's touch to the churning fear when she'd first been taken, and then the overwhelming shock, like a tidal wave of numbness, when she'd realised the colossal mistake they'd both made.

Zayed glanced back at her, his expression closed, his eyes hard. 'Are you holding up?' he asked brusquely, and Olivia nodded, knowing she shouldn't be touched by such a small, simple question, yet feeling it all the same. Tears stung her eyes and she blinked them back fiercely. The last thing she wanted to do now was cry. She didn't even know what she'd be crying for— for what she was about to lose, or what she'd already lost?

They rode in silence, bumping over dunes for

two hours, until they came to a huddle of Bedouin tents by a small oasis fringed with palms. Even before the Jeep came to a stop outside the circle of tents Olivia could feel the sense of desolation and despair. It hung like a mist over the camp, a darkness despite the sun that glinted diamond-bright off rock and boulders in the distance.

Zayed leapt out of the Jeep in one graceful movement and then, to Olivia's surprise, he reached behind and held out his hand for her. Olivia took it, the feel of his rough, callused palm on hers reminding her of how he'd touched her earlier, and how she'd responded to it.

It seemed incredible that she could be affected by him even now, with confusion all around them, but her body felt as if it were supernaturally attuned to his. Or was she just naïve because no man had ever paid her any attention before? Either way, she had to ignore the fizzing sensation in her stomach, the electric excitement that pulsed through her as his hand brushed hers.

'Come.' Zayed dropped her hand once she'd exited the Jeep and Olivia followed him into the camp. Men, women and children milled about in states of sadness and anxiety; after speaking to some of the leaders, Zayed told Olivia that Malouf's men had raided the camp and stolen their goats and camels, roughed up a few of their men. A few of the women and children were hurt, collateral damage, but fortunately no one had been too badly injured.

'It could have been worse,' Zayed said grimly, his expression making Olivia think that he had seen worse before, more than once.

'Let me help,' she said. 'Where are the women and children who have been hurt?'

Zayed nodded towards the tranquil pool of water the camp had been built around. 'They are washing in the oasis.'

Nodding, Olivia started towards the group of women she saw huddled by the pool. She didn't know exactly what she could do to help, only that she wanted to be of some use. Her heart ached for these people, the confusion they felt at having their home so needlessly destroyed.

The women turned as she approached, eyes narrowing with curiosity, and Olivia wondered how on earth she could explain who she was. But then, for better or worse, it turned out there was no explanation needed.

'I...help,' she said haltingly, and a child ran towards her, tackling her around the knees. Relief poured through her. Until that moment she hadn't quite realised how much she needed to feel useful. To be needed.

She spent the next few hours bandaging cuts

and cleaning scrapes, communicating in a mixture of halting Arabic and miming that made the children chortle with glee.

Olivia soon realised that the way she could be the most useful was simply by listening and chatting to the women and children, distracting them from their worries. And, goodness knew, she could use some distraction as well.

When all the injuries had been seen to, they retired to one of the women's tents, drank apricot juice and nibbled on pitta bread with fresh hummus.

Before long she had a chubby baby on her hip and a toddler clinging to her legs as the women began firing questions at her, only half of which Olivia could understand, and none of which she could answer.

Who was she? Was she Zayed's bride? Had he married in secret? Were they in love? When Olivia blushed, the woman crowed with laughter, delighted by her response. Even when she said nothing, it seemed she gave something away. And, with dread curdling in her stomach, she had a feeling Zayed would be furious.

But perhaps he would be furious with her, no matter what. He seemed determined to be, just as he was determined to regain what he'd lost. She would just be collateral damage, so much jetsam to be thrown away. The thought made her throat close. It hurt to be so disregarded, even though part of her understood it. Really, what else could she expect? Prince Zayed had a country to think of. She was just one woman, an unimportant palace servant he needed to get rid of.

'Come.' One of the women smiled at her and plucked her sleeve. 'You are tired. You rest.'

She was tired, every muscle and sinew pulsing with exhaustion. With a smile of relieved gratitude, Olivia followed the woman to another tent where she could sleep…and perhaps forget, for a little while, the mess she was still hopelessly embroiled in.

It had been a strange, surreal kind of day. Zayed had been immersed in meetings with the tribal leaders, listening to their complaints, assuring them he would have vengeance on Malouf's men. He'd already sent one of his own patrols out after the raiders, in the hope of recapturing the tribe's valuable livestock. He saw the hope and, far more damning, the faith in the eyes of his people when he spoke to them and guilt cramped his stomach. How could they trust him as their leader, when he'd made such an enormous mistake? When he'd married the wrong woman and put his country's most valuable alliance at terrible risk?

Even though he barely saw her, Zayed was conscious of Olivia throughout the day. He saw her down at the oasis, washing and bandaging the children's scrapes with meticulous care. Later, when all the injuries had been seen to, he saw her laughing and playing in the water, kids crawling over her. The women seemed to have accepted her into their fold without question, which made Zayed wonder if they assumed she was his bride. Did they know she wasn't the woman he'd meant to have? He had no idea if Olivia's rudimentary Arabic was up to the task of disabusing them of any of their assumptions...or if she even would. Perhaps she was simply making herself useful so he would see what an asset she could be to him.

He shouldn't have brought her, he supposed, so he could have stemmed any questions or curiosity, but he hadn't thought the news of his bride would have spread to such a remote place. And he hadn't wanted to let Olivia out of his sight, not until he knew what he was going to do with her.

In late afternoon, as the shadows started drawing in, Zayed met with Jahmal.

'We'll stay the night,' he informed his aide. 'And leave in the morning for Rubyhan.'

Jahmal raised his eyebrows. 'Rubyhan? Is that wise?'

Zayed took a deep breath and let it out slowly. 'I need to retrench and decide what I am going to do about Olivia.' Rubyhan, the summer palace of the royal family of Kalidar, had thankfully remained in his possession throughout Malouf's reign. He used it as the seat of his provisional government and the place to which he went when he needed to regroup. And he certainly needed to regroup now.

A headache flickered at his temples and Zayed closed his eyes, fighting the pain. The last thing he needed was one of the crippling migraines he'd suffered from since receiving a head injury eight years ago in one of the battles against Malouf's men.

'My Prince?' Jahmal sounded cautious. 'Surely you can simply set her aside? She is only a servant.'

Irritation prickled his scalp and tightened his gut at the suggestion, although it was no more than what he'd already thought himself. Yet somehow he didn't like his aide saying it.

'It is not so simple,' he said tightly. 'Sultan Hassan will have realised I kidnapped his servant and, moreover, that I intended to kidnap his daughter. Our negotiations will be thrown into total disarray.' If not broken off completely. 'I need to mend things with Hassan. When I

have an answer from him, I can decide what to
do about Olivia.'

'Still,' Jahmal persisted. 'It can be managed.
If she is only a servant…'

Only a servant.

It was true, of course. Olivia was, to all in-
tents and purposes, expendable. So why did
that thought bother him right now? It shouldn't,
Zayed realised with sudden, crystalline clarity. He was letting sentiment cloud his vision,
soften his determination. Despite his suspicions,
he felt guilty for the way he'd treated her last
night, so he was resisting the prospect of setting her aside and what it would mean for her.
But he couldn't let last night change things. He
couldn't let Olivia matter at all.

'I do not wish to discuss it now,' he said in a
clipped voice. 'I am going to wash and then we
will eat with the tribal leaders.'

'Very good, My Prince.'

Later, after he'd washed and eaten, he went in
search of Olivia. He hadn't seen her for several
hours, and the realisation made unease deepen
within his chest, although he couldn't say why.

One of the women informed him she'd been
given her own tent, which confirmed his suspicions that the tribe knew she was a woman of
importance, perhaps even his bride. He really
shouldn't have brought her. His judgement was

being clouded again and again, it seemed. The sooner this woman was out of his life, the better.

He bent to enter her tent, the flap falling closed behind him. He straightened, glancing around at the rough furnishings, a far cry from the sumptuous luxury she'd had back at his own camp. She was sitting on a pallet covered with sheepskin, her slender fingers flying as they plaited her damp hair. Her eyes widened as she saw him come in but she said nothing, just watched him warily.

Zayed's gaze flicked over her. She wore the same nondescript tunic and trousers she'd been in earlier, hardly clothes to inflame a man, yet even now he felt that inexorable pull to her. What was it about this woman? She wasn't anything special. Yes, her eyes were lovely, and her figure was appealing, but she was just a woman. One among many, although he hadn't had a woman for a long time before Olivia. Perhaps that was it. He'd denied himself carnal pleasures for too long, in pursuit of his inheritance. His kingdom.

'Tomorrow we are travelling to Rubyhan.'

'Rubyhan?'

'The summer palace of the royal family and the seat of my government.'

She nodded slowly, finishing her plait before resting her hands in her lap. 'And then?'

'Then I will contact Sultan Hassan, and you will write the letter.'

'And when I do? What are you hoping will happen?'

'That he will understand the mistake I made and we will reopen marriage negotiations.' Anything else was intolerable, impossible. He had to have Hassan's support in fighting Malouf. For the last ten years various political leaders had tried to distance themselves from Kalidar's civil war, waiting to see the outcome. On several occasions he had been on the precipice of victory; once he'd made it to the capital city of Arjah, only to have the palace gates closed against him.

With Hassan's support, he could exert political pressure on Malouf and force him to resign. The man was old, with no heirs; his soldiers were starting to dissent, tired of the endless fighting against Zayed and his men, knowing him to be the rightful King. A bloodless coup would be the perfect victory and finally, finally, an end to all the war and loss.

Olivia nodded slowly, her head bent, her gaze on her clasped hands. Zayed could see the nape of her neck, the tender skin, the pale, curling hairs, and the sight caused a nameless feeling to clench his insides in a way he didn't like. 'And what will happen to me, do you suppose?' she asked after a moment.

'Are you hoping for a settlement?'

She looked up, eyes flashing. 'You sound so judgemental.'

'I was merely asking a question.'

'No, you weren't.' She took a quick, shuddering breath. 'You have judged me again and again for falling into bed with you. I admit, it was a mistake. A colossal mistake. But I didn't mean to do it. If I could undo it, I would. I have no desire to be your Queen. I have never been interested in power or money.' Another quick breath tore at his senses. He had a bizarre urge to comfort her, even though he knew he couldn't.

'All I've wanted,' Olivia continued more quietly, 'is a place to belong. A sense of family. A job to do. I had all that with the royal family of Abkar.'

'And so you will have it again.'

She glanced at him, scorn clear on her face, surprising him. 'Now you are the one who is naïve.'

'What do you mean?'

'It doesn't matter.'

'No, tell me.' Zayed took a step towards her. 'What do you mean? What do you think will happen to you when you return to Abkar?'

'Why do you care?' Olivia challenged. 'You have not been all that interested in my welfare, Prince Zayed.'

He stiffened with affront. 'I told you, I am a man of honour.'

'I have yet to see any evidence of that,' Olivia said quietly. It was her tone that got to him. She wasn't angry or accusing. No, she was merely stating a fact. And, with a rush of churning regret, he realised it was true.

'You must understand why I have to be suspicious,' he said after a pause. 'So much is at stake. There is no one I can trust.'

She arched an eyebrow. 'What do you think I am going to do? Perform some act of sabotage? I am not some spy for Malouf.'

His blood chilled to hear it so plainly. He would not put such a preposterous idea beyond the wily fiend…but he didn't think Olivia was part of such a nefarious plan. Nor, he realised, did he think she was scheming to better her position. He'd seen too much despair and shock from her to believe that any longer, even if it would have made it easier to plot his own course with no consideration of the woman before him.

'I know you are not a spy,' he said gruffly. 'But I must be careful.'

'I understand.' Now she simply sounded tired. 'And tomorrow I will write your wretched letter and hopefully all of this will go away. Or at least I will.' She glanced at him, her expression filled with weariness. 'Now I'd like to go to bed, if you don't mind.'

Zayed stared at her, wishing he'd got more answers. What would happen to her when she returned to Abkar? He could settle money on her, enough to make sure she would need nothing for a long time. Fortunately he'd been able to secure the royal family's personal investments before Malouf had taken control, which were considerable. He didn't want for money, and he could make sure Olivia didn't either.

But was it enough? And why were such things bothering him now? He glanced at her, at the slight shoulders bowed under an invisible weight, that tender nape. Her lashes swept her cheeks in sooty fans as she lowered her gaze, waiting for him to go.

But he didn't want to. Quite suddenly he could remember the exact feel and taste of her. He could recall how pliant she'd been in his arms, and how exquisite it had felt to be sheathed inside her. Inconvenient memories that made his body stir with insistent desire.

'Please let me know if there is anything you need,' he said finally, shifting to ease the ache in his groin. 'I'm sorry your accommodation is not more comfortable.'

'It's fine, and more than I expected from somewhere so remote.' She didn't look at him, merely stretched out on the pallet, waiting for him leave, ready for sleep.

Zayed hesitated another second. This was his bride, whether he wanted her or not, whether he'd meant it or not. He might set her aside as soon as possible, but for now she was his responsibility, and he felt the weight of it with sudden, inexplicable fierceness.

Yet at the moment she wanted nothing from him. She refused even to look at him. And so, filled with a restless unease, Zayed bid her goodnight and left the tent.

CHAPTER SEVEN

THEY LEFT FOR Rubyhan early the next morning. The sky was a pale, luminescent pink as Olivia climbed into the Jeep, gazing around at the harsh desert landscape transformed momentarily into softness and light as dawn broke over the dunes.

She'd spent four years in Abkar, on the edge of the desert, but she'd rarely ventured into its barren heart. If she wasn't at the palace, then she was accompanying the Princess on various holidays, mostly to Europe or the Caribbean, playgrounds of the rich and royal.

Prince Zayed was an entirely different kind of royal, she mused as she watched him swing up into the Jeep, his muscles rippling with the graceful movement. He reminded her of some ancient warrior, proud and defiant and definitely dangerous. He wasn't like the pampered aristos she'd seen on some of her travels with the royal family, partying it up, whinging about whatever they could. No, she couldn't see Prince Zayed at some Monte Carlo night club. He was too raw and primal for that, and even now she was drawn to him.

Yesterday, as she'd helped the women and children, her gaze had been drawn to him again and again. Drawn to his powerful form, and also the way he spoke and listened, the intense responsibility he felt for his people, his country. She'd had the sudden, crazy thought that, when Prince Zayed did love a woman, it would be with that same blazing focus. It just wouldn't be her.

Now his grey-green gaze caught and snared hers and Olivia looked away, afraid her thoughts would be written on her face. Why on earth was she thinking about whom he might love? Their one night together had awakened a longing inside her she'd managed to suppress until now. And she had to keep suppressing it. The last thing she wanted to do was feel something—something more—for Zayed.

She'd thought they would be taking the Jeep to Rubyhan, but after an hour's travel they reached a helipad on a flat plain, the horizon stretching out to nowhere in every direction.

'We're going by helicopter?' Olivia asked, even though she supposed it was obvious.

Zayed nodded. 'Rubyhan is unreachable by

any other means. It will take an hour by helicopter.' Anything else he said was cut off by
the whirring of blades as a helicopter appeared
on the horizon, coming closer. Olivia put her
hands over her ears as the sand kicked up and
the military helicopter landed.

Zayed opened the door and held out his hand
to help her climb up. She took it, conscious of
the strength of his grip as he hoisted her inside.
She buckled herself into one of the seats, feeling
the surrealness of the situation all over again.
How could she be in a helicopter in the middle
of the desert with a prince? And yet she was.

Zayed climbed in after her, settling into the
seat next to her, then his aide who had told him
about the attack. The door closed and the craft
lifted into the air, the desert dropping away beneath them.

Olivia craned her neck to look out of the window as they sped towards the horizon. From
above the desert looked tranquil, the undulating
dunes smooth and graceful, belying how rugged and dangerous the landscape truly could
be.

After a little while a mountain range rose up
in front of them, jagged peaks piercing the blue
sky. The helicopter began to descend, the pilot
navigating his way through the ferocious-look-
ing peaks, making Olivia press back in her seat.

Out of the window she could see snow-covered mountains adorned with shreds of cloud, almost close enough to touch.

And then the palace was in front of them, like something out of a fairy tale, its walls emerging from the rock as if they had been hewn from it, each one topped with a bright, domed minaret.

'Wow.' She breathed, and Zayed turned to her with a small smile.

'It is impressive, is it not? Built six hundred years ago by my ancestor.'

'I've never seen its equal.'

'It is called the Palace of Clouds. Rubyhan is its formal name only.'

'It is a palace of clouds,' Olivia said with a little laugh. 'I can't believe how high we are. I saw snow.'

'Yes, it will be far colder here,' Zayed warned her.

'How long will we be here?'

Zayed's mouth thinned. 'A few days only,' he answered, and Olivia's stomach did a little nervous flip. A few days…and then what?

After they landed Zayed escorted her into the palace; the interior was just as incredible as the outside: rooms with soaring windows and balconies that overlooked the stunning vista, the ground dropping away to nothing immediately beyond the walls.

'You will stay in the former harem,' he told her. 'I think you will be very comfortable.'

The harem was a suite of rooms with every luxury to hand: a huge bedroom with a king-sized bed on its own dais; an en-suite bathroom with a sunken marble tub, an infinity shower and underfloor heating. A balcony extended from the bedroom, making Olivia feel as if she was walking on thin air. She could hardly believe all the luxuries found in such a remote place—it was even more sumptuous a palace than the one she knew in Abkar.

Zayed left her there, telling her to rest and relax, and after a few moments of uncertainty Olivia decided to take him at his word. It had been a harrowing few days, and she could certainly use the opportunity to relax, especially considering how rarely she did it.

Her days at the palace in Abkar were taken up with caring for the three young Princesses— teaching them English, keeping them in line, managing their lessons, their social calendars, their wardrobes. Olivia hardly took any holiday—she never needed to. Where would she go? Besides a godmother in Paris she saw every few years, she had no one in the world.

And if she lost her position in Abkar, which she was almost certain she would, she'd have nowhere to go. But she couldn't think about that yet. She was going to take one day at a time, one hour if necessary, and right now she was going to revel in a lovely, long soak in the sunken tub, which was a far cry from the cool water of the oasis where she'd last washed, the bottom slimy with seaweed and mud.

She'd just got out of the bath, wrapping herself in the velvet-soft terry-cloth robe that had been hanging on the bathroom door, when there was a discreet knock on the door of the suite.

'Miss Taylor?' The voice was female and had a crisp English accent, which filled Olivia with relief. She'd been managing all right with Arabic, and Zayed's English was flawless, but it would be nice to have someone else to converse with in the language of her birth.

'Yes, just a moment.' She opened the door to a young woman dressed in a business suit, her dark hair pulled back in a sleek ponytail. Olivia liked the look of her instinctively. 'Hello.'

'Hello, Miss Taylor.'

'Please, call me Olivia.'

The woman smiled and nodded. 'I'm Anna, Prince Zayed's PA at Rubyhan. He's asked me to make sure you have everything you need.'

'Yes, it's been rather amazing.' Olivia let out a self-conscious laugh, aware she was in nothing but a dressing gown. 'I just got out of the bath.'

'And I hope you enjoyed it,' Anna said

smoothly. 'Prince Zayed wishes your stay here to be as pleasant as possible.'

It sounded a little…formal. 'Oh. Okay.' Olivia tried for a smile. Zayed was being thoughtful for once; she should be pleased. So why did she feel uneasy, as if she was being managed? Dealt with?

'So there is nothing you need?' Anna pressed, and Olivia shook her head.

'Then Prince Zayed asks that you join him for dinner in the Blue Room in an hour. Is that acceptable to you?'

Olivia tried to suppress the flutter of nerves and, yes, excitement she felt at the prospect. 'Um, yes. Sure. Thank you.'

'Good.' Anna smiled. 'I believe that the wardrobe in your suite should hold any clothes you might need, but please do alert me if you require anything further.' She handed Olivia a pager. 'If you push that button, I'll be here in less than five minutes.'

'Oh. Wow.' Olivia had never experienced such service before. She'd never experienced *anything* like this before. It really was out of this world. Out of her world.

'I'll leave you to it, then,' Anna said with a smile. 'When you're ready for dinner, press the pager and I'll escort you to the Blue Room.'

'Okay. Thanks.'

Anna left her alone and, feeling a mix of curiosity and trepidation, Olivia opened the louvre doors of the huge built-in wardrobe. A row of blouses, skirts and dresses in every imaginable shade and fabric greeted and amazed her.

She ran her finger along the garments, touching the sumptuous fabrics, from cotton and linen to silk and satin. Beneath the dresses were shoes of every description—high heels and sandals, court shoes and plimsolls. They all looked incredibly expensive. Olivia slid open one of the drawers built into the wardrobe and nearly gasped at the delicate garments laid out there—lingerie sets in shades of ivory and beige, scalloped with lace and as thin as gossamer. Why on earth did Zayed have all these women's clothes here? How had he got them here so quickly?

She spent an enjoyable half hour trying on different outfits, from the evening gowns to the day dresses, knowing she wouldn't dare to wear anything too extravagant or sexy. She finally settled on a simply cut sheath in royal-blue linen, pairing it with a pair of taupe court shoes. Simple, safe clothes that were still more expensive and elegant than anything she'd ever worn before.

It felt strange, to be dressed so nicely, waiting to have dinner with a man she barely knew, yet who she'd known more than any other man in her life. Strange, and more than a little bit exciting.

'There is absolutely no reason to be looking forward to this,' Olivia told her reflection as she put on the minimum of make-up—the bathroom came equipped with a dazzling array of cosmetics and toiletries. 'No reason at all. Prince Zayed no doubt just wants to talk to you about dissolving this marriage.'

The reminder was timely and squelched some of that nervy excitement. This was a business meeting, and one she certainly shouldn't be looking forward to.

Taking a deep breath, she pressed the pager. Minutes later, as promised, Anna appeared at her door and led her down several corridors with mosaic floors and Moorish arches to a room on the ground floor of the palace. She opened the door and stepped aside so Olivia could enter, which she did with her heart starting to jump around in her chest.

But she needn't have been so nervous, because the room, stunning as it was, was empty. Anna closed the doors softly behind her and Olivia looked around, taking in the pillars decorated with lapis lazuli and the gold leaf on the walls and ceiling. In the centre of the room a table for two had been set with linen and crystal and flickered with candlelight. It looked rather romantic, Olivia couldn't help but think.

Then the doors opened and Zayed stood there, freshly showered and shaven, dressed in western-fashion trousers and a matching charcoal-grey button-down shirt open at the throat. His eyes shone like pieces of agate as his gaze surveyed her. He looked absolutely devastating, and Olivia couldn't form so much as a word as she stood there like a rabbit in a snare.

Zayed closed the doors behind him with a soft click and came forward. 'Hello, Olivia,' he said.

Zayed watched the pulse flutter and leap in Olivia's throat as he walked towards her. He was reminded of their wedding night, when he'd seen how nervous she was and he'd tried to relax her. Tonight was different, though. Yes, he was trying to make her comfortable after everything she'd endured, but he had no intention of seducing her...as tempting as that prospect seemed at the moment.

'Everything in your suite was to your satisfaction?' he asked.

'Yes.' Olivia cleared her throat and gave him a nervous smile. 'It was all amazing, thank you.'

'I'm glad.' He pulled out her chair and she sat down, bending her head so he could see the nape of her neck, and just as before he was struck by the tender vulnerability of it. Struck in a way he did not wish to be.

'It's incredible, all the luxuries here,' Olivia continued as Zayed moved around to sit opposite her. 'The bath…the underfloor heating… the clothes…' She shook her head, marvelling. 'How did you get so many clothes here so quickly, and most of them in my size?'

Zayed hesitated a second too long, and realisation darkened Olivia's eyes to a deep navy. 'Oh, how stupid of me,' she said with an uneven little laugh. 'They were here already, weren't they? For Princess Halina.'

Her perception was razor-sharp and Zayed couldn't deny it. 'I was intending to bring her here afterwards,' he said. 'A honeymoon of sorts.'

'How lovely.' Olivia reached for her napkin and spread it in her lap, her head bent so he couldn't see her expression.

Annoyance and something deeper stabbed through him. He had been looking forward to this evening, even though it would have its expedient uses, of course. Now, right at the beginning, it felt spoiled somehow, which was absurd. Halina would still be his wife. She had to be. And Olivia's perception provided a timely reminder.

'I hope you were able to relax and enjoy yourself.'

'I was, thank you.' She sounded cool, and Zayed gritted his teeth. He wasn't even sure why he was so irritated.

'Have some wine,' he said, and reached for the bottle chilling in a silver bucket. Olivia lifted her gaze to his, a slightly teasing look lightening the blue of her eyes, reminding him of the sea.

'I didn't think you experienced all this luxury in your exile,' she confessed as he filled her glass. 'I thought you lived in a tent pretty much all the time.'

'Mostly I do. But Rubyhan is my official base and the seat of my government.'

'So Anna works for your government?'

'She is my personal assistant, but yes, I have a small staff living here permanently arranging correspondence, managing affairs. Although I am in exile, I am still the globally recognised leader of Kalidar. It is Malouf who is the rebel, the impostor.' A familiar pressure started in his chest.

'I know that,' Olivia said quietly. She took a sip of her wine, her lashes lowered. 'It must be very difficult to be fighting for so long.'

'I want the fighting to be over.' The ache in his chest intensified and came out in his voice. 'I want innocent people to suffer no more.'

'And your marriage to Princess Halina will help accomplish that,' Olivia finished softly.

'Yes.' He paused, feeling the need suddenly to explain to her why he was so committed. 'For ten years Fakhir Malouf has lived in my home and taken my place. But worse than that, far worse, he has implemented policies and laws that go against everything my father taught me as a ruler—justice and mercy, kindness and equality. Kalidar was one of the most forward-thinking nations in this region, and now it is one of the least, all thanks to Malouf.'

'But why doesn't someone intervene—another government?'

Zayed's fingers clenched around the stem of his wine glass and he forced himself to relax. 'We are a small if wealthy country, and no one has wanted to risk getting involved. Malouf had the support of a certain section of the military, and it gave him more clout, even if no one was willing to recognise him officially.'

'So for ten years you have been living on the fringes,' Olivia said with a little shake of her head. 'It's so terribly unfair.'

'It is an injustice I will make right, even if it costs me my life. Nothing else matters.' He held her gaze, willing her to understand. He couldn't let himself care about her finer feelings.

'I understand,' Olivia said softly, and Zayed let out a low breath, accepting her response.

He leaned back in his chair, wanting to recapture some of the enjoyment of the evening. He was sitting with a beautiful woman in candlelight, drinking smooth, velvety wine. Nothing could happen between them, for both their sakes, but they could still have a pleasant time together.

'So tell me about yourself, Olivia,' he invited as a member of his staff slipped into the room quietly to serve them the first course of lamb *sambousek* with fresh cucumber sauce.

'Tell you…?' Olivia looked startled. 'There is not much to know, I'm afraid.'

'That can't be true.' Zayed realised he was curious about her. 'You said you had been working for the royal family since you were seventeen?'

'Eighteen. Right after I finished school.'

'You went to boarding school?'

'Yes, in Switzerland. My father moved around a great deal and he wanted me to have a stable education.'

'Did you enjoy it?'

She shrugged. 'It was a finishing school for aristocrats and princesses, and I was a minor diplomat's daughter, a nobody. I was there on a scholarship,' she explained. 'And of course everyone knew it, since I didn't fly in by helicopter, or wear designer clothes on the weekends, or keep my own pony.' She let out a small laugh that sounded just a bit too sad. 'Halina was my best friend,' Olivia continued. 'She took me under her wing, made sure other people didn't tease me.' But not being teased, Zayed acknowledged silently, wasn't the same as being liked.

'That was very kind of her.'

'Yes, it was. She's a very giving person.' She took a quick breath, looking up at him uncertainly. 'I hope things are able to work out between you.'

'So do I.' Yet it felt odd in a way he couldn't elucidate to talk about Halina as his wife. He didn't want to talk about Halina right now, didn't even want to think about her. Not with Olivia sitting across from him and looking so very lovely. If that was an act of betrayal, so be it.

'This letter,' Olivia said slowly. 'What exactly do you want me to say in it?'

He didn't want to talk about the letter now, either. 'There is time for that tomorrow,' he said swiftly. 'Why don't we eat?'

Olivia nodded and took a small bite of the *sambousek*, fragrant with cinnamon and mint. 'Delicious,' she murmured. 'Better than any I've tasted before.'

'Tell me about your duties in Abkar,' Zayed

suggested. He wanted to know more about her, although he knew there was no real reason to. 'You take care of the three younger Princesses?' He didn't know their names.

'Yes, Saddah, Maarit and Aisha. They are twelve, ten and eight.'

'And what do you do?'

'Everything,' Olivia answered with a small smile. 'I'm meant to teach them English, but I also look after their belongings and arrange their lessons and social events. They are quite busy girls. Dancing, riding, tennis... Saddah will go to boarding school, the same one I went to, next year.'

She lapsed into silence, her face drawn into sorrowful lines that made Zayed lean forward and touch her hand. 'What is it? Why do you look sad suddenly?'

She refocused on him with a wry smile that was still touched with sadness. 'I'll miss them, that's all.'

'But you can return to the palace in Abkar when all this is over,' Zayed insisted. 'I will make sure of it.'

'I am not sure you will be able to arrange such a thing,' Olivia answered quietly. 'Sultan Hassan has entrusted me with the care of his precious daughters. I'm meant to be an example of womanhood to them—quiet, submissive, modest womanhood.' Her lips twisted. 'No matter how discreetly things are managed, word will get back to him and to them that...' She gestured between them with one slender hand. 'I have compromised myself.'

Zayed's mouth thinned into a hard line. 'And in the letter, we can explain that it was not your fault.'

'And have you take the blame? That would jeopardise your marriage negotiations, surely?'

Yes, it would. Zayed stared at her in frustration, disliking how he'd put her in such an untenable position. After the events of the last few days, he realised how unfounded his suspicions were.

Olivia was not a scheming gold-digger, trying to get the most out of this unfortunate arrangement. It would have been easier to maintain such a fiction, but he couldn't, not when he'd seen her help the women and children at the camp; not when she'd shown so much concern for his welfare as well as that of his country.

'Still,' he persisted. 'I will give you a handsome settlement. You will want for nothing.'

'That is very generous of you, Prince Zayed.' But she didn't sound entirely pleased by the prospect, and he didn't understand why.

'You could travel,' he continued, determined

that she see some benefits. 'Or start over. Work somewhere new.'

'Yes.' She laid down her fork, her appetite seemingly gone.

'Does none of that appeal to you?'

'It's only…' She sighed. 'Abkar has been my home for four years, the only home I've ever really known. Sultan Hassan is my employer, I know, but he's been kind to me, and more like a father than my own, who I barely knew. I'll miss that.'

So not only had he robbed her of her innocence and livelihood, but he'd taken her family and home as well. Guilt corroded his insides like acid. There had to be some way he could make this right.

CHAPTER EIGHT

OLIVIA TOOK IN the frown settled between Zayed's straight, dark brows and wondered what he was so worried about. What did it matter to him if she travelled or got a new job? Or was she simply a burden to his conscience, and it would be far easier for him if she quite happily toddled off into whatever future remained for her?

'I'd like to travel,' Olivia said, injecting a note of enthusiasm into her voice that she didn't quite feel. 'I'd like to go to Paris. My godmother lives there.'

'Your godmother?' Olivia saw the unmistakeable relief on Zayed's face and knew she had been right. He wanted her dealt with, taken care of.

'Yes, an old friend of my mother's. I haven't seen her in years. It will be good to see her again.' Which wasn't quite true. Her godmother was elderly and practically a stranger, and she'd welcomed Olivia during her few, brief visits with a sense of obligation rather than enthusiasm. But Olivia knew what Zayed wanted to hear, and it was her instinct, as ever, to say it. Whether it was her father having needed to be reassured that she was fine at school, or Halina that she didn't mind it when she went off with other friends, or even the little Princesses, needing to be soothed and petted, Olivia couldn't help but give people what they wanted. It was so much easier, and being useful was almost as good as being loved.

Zayed gazed at her, eyes narrowed, the relief fading from his face. 'Why are you trying to make me feel better?'

His perception surprised her. 'You don't want to worry about me. You don't have to.'

'You're my responsibility.'

'Not really.' She met his gaze levelly. 'And, as for money, I don't need any. I have savings of my own and I'd prefer not to be paid off.' Just the thought of accepting money from him after everything they'd done together made her feel cheap. Cheaper than she already felt.

Zayed shook his head. 'Like I said, I have a responsibility—'

'And I'm absolving you of it.' Olivia managed a smile even though her heart felt as though it were being wrung out like a sponge. She understood she couldn't stay with Zayed; she didn't even want to, not really. But neither did she feel confident or courageous enough to embrace the unknown future. 'At least you don't think I'm some scheming witch any more,' she said lightly, 'trying to trick you into staying married to me.'

He had the grace to look abashed. 'I'm sorry. I have come to realise that was unfair of me.'

'When did you realise that?'

'Over time,' he said slowly. 'When I saw you helping at the settlement yesterday. Or perhaps the way you seemed to care more for my situation, my people, than you did for yourself.'

His admiring words caused a warm glow to start inside her. 'You have a lot more at stake, Zayed. Plenty of people are your responsibility, so I don't need to be one of them.'

He didn't look convinced, and Olivia decided it was time to change the subject. There was only so much reassuring she could do, especially when the truth was the thought of her unknown future made her stomach churn. She didn't have that much in savings; Sultan Hassan paid her a pittance because she was also given food and board. Her employment skills were limited to being some kind of governess, but she'd hardly get a reference from the Sultan.

And what if she was pregnant?

That was a possibility she hadn't let herself

dwell on. Zayed hadn't seemed to have considered it, although perhaps it was simply not of concern to him. Despite his seeming solicitude now, she knew she shouldn't entirely trust him, even if she wanted to, and she doubted he trusted her. What would he do if she *was* pregnant? She didn't even like to think about it.

'What's wrong?' Zayed asked suddenly. 'You've gone pale.'

'Nothing.' She'd been meaning to change the subject, so now she did. 'This meal is really quite delicious. What is the main course?'

'I have no idea.' Zayed pressed a pager to summon the staff. 'But we can find out.'

Moments later a member of staff came in and silently removed the dishes, returning shortly with the main course—grilled meat with rice and yoghurt sauce. Again it was delicious, and Olivia said so, but she knew she couldn't just keep talking about the food.

And Zayed, for whatever reason, seemed determined to find out more about her. 'What kind of job might you have done, if Hassan hadn't offered you the governess position?'

Olivia shook her head. 'I never really thought about it.'

'Did you consider going to university?'

'No, not really.'

Zayed frowned. 'Not even for a moment?

In this day and age…an educated woman like yourself… Why not?'

She pressed her lips together. 'There wasn't the money for it.'

His frown deepened, turning almost to a scowl. 'No money? Did your father leave you nothing?'

'He died virtually bankrupt.' He'd had a penchant for gambling that Olivia hadn't known about, and there had barely been enough to cover her most basic expenses after the funeral. 'I didn't really feel like going to university,' she told him, wanting to avoid his pity. 'I didn't have a burning passion to study anything, and the truth is I'm not very adventurous.' The thought of starting over alone in a strange city had been most unappealing. She'd done that enough as a child, before she'd been sent to boarding school at age eleven.

'And what about now?' Zayed pressed. 'If you could do anything, what would you do?'

'I…' Olivia hesitated. She didn't have dreams. She hadn't let herself have them, because they'd seemed so pointless. Better to be happy pleasing other people, accepting their thanks when it came. Better to be useful than important or loved.

'Think about it,' Zayed urged. 'This could be a great opportunity for you, Olivia.'

A great opportunity? Olivia blinked, stung.

She understood about putting a good face on things, heaven knew, but that was stretching it a little far.

'I'm sorry, Prince Zayed,' she said stiffly. 'But I can't quite see that from where I am.' She put her napkin next to her plate, her appetite vanished.

What was she doing here, really? Having a romantic candlelit dinner with a man who was going to put her aside so he could marry someone else? A man who had taken her innocence, her livelihood, her *home*. Did she have anything more to lose? The last thing she needed was to sit here, eating delicious food and drinking fine wine, as if they were on some sort of date. It just reminded her of all she didn't have, would never have, and, while she usually didn't let herself think like that, right now it hurt.

Because part of her wanted that—the romance, the anticipation, the seduction—with Zayed. She didn't want to feel that persistent ache of yearning, but she did. He was a powerful and devastatingly attractive man, and despite his ruthlessness she knew he could be kind. It was enough right there to half tumble her into love with him, and that she could not have.

'I'm sorry,' she said as she rose from the table. 'It's been a long day. I think I'll go to bed.'

'Olivia, wait.' Zayed rose as well, catching

her arm and turning her towards him. A wave of heat, the tangy citrus of his aftershave, assaulted her senses and felt like a taunt. Even now she felt the ripples of desire spreading outwards from her centre, like a pebble had splashed into her soul, and she couldn't stand it.

She didn't want to want him. Didn't want to long for things she couldn't have, to yearn to feel those strong arms around her, pulling her against him, and more. So much more.

'I'm sorry,' Zayed said, his hand still on her arm. 'That was a poor choice of words. I'm trying to see the bright side of things for you, but I understand that there docsn't seem to be one at the moment. Please stay and finish the meal with me.'

Olivia knew she should tug her arm away from Zayed and keep walking out the door. Protect herself rather than let herself ache and yearn. But somehow she couldn't. She wasn't strong enough, and the thought of going back to her room and spending the rest of the evening alone made loneliness swamp her.

So she nodded and Zayed released her arm, a small smile flitting across his features.

'Thank you,' he murmured, and they both sat down.

It had been a stupid thing to say. Zayed saw that now. He saw it in Olivia's pale face, in how her hands were not quite steady as she spread her napkin across her lap. He'd been trying to make her feel better and it hadn't worked.

Hell, he realised, he'd been trying to make himself feel better. Because guilt was an emotion he couldn't afford to feel. If Olivia could get something out of what had happened, if she could benefit, then he'd feel better about putting her aside.

The fact that he even needed such a sop to his conscience filled him with fury—and shame. For ten years he had let himself think of nothing but duty, fuelled by grief. When he closed his eyes, he saw the tormented face of his mother, dying simply because she had no more wish to live. He saw the helicopter in flames. He heard the anguished cries and shouts of his father and brother, even though he knew that was only in his imagination. It would have been impossible to hear over the sound of the blades and the flames. The headache he'd been trying to suppress for the last forty-eight hours flickered insistently at his temples.

He could not believe how weak and sentimental he was being. Why was he trying to make this woman, who meant so little, feel better? That was why he'd brought her to Rubyhan, Zayed realised with another rush of shame. Why he'd given her the sumptuous suite, the clothes. Why he was wining and dining her tonight.

Although that wasn't quite true. No, it was worse than that—he was wining and dining her because he wanted to. Because he'd wanted to see her, be with her. Because even now, with so much at stake, he still desired this slip of a woman who should be completely forgettable to him. *Why?*

'Zayed…?' Olivia glanced at him uncertainly. 'It's late and I am sure you have many things to do tomorrow. Maybe I should go…'

She started to rise again, but Zayed stayed her with one upturned palm. He took a deep breath, willing the pain in his head to recede. 'No.'

'You seem…' She hesitated. 'Angry.'

'I am angry at myself,' Zayed confessed. Olivia gazed at him in confusion.

'You mean for marrying me by mistake?'

'Yes, that.' His mouth twisted in something like a smile. 'But also for wanting you even now, when I know I shouldn't.'

It was as if he'd stolen all the air from the room in a single breath. Olivia froze, her eyes wide and stormy, her pink lips parted.

'You do?'

'Can you not feel it, Olivia? Why do you think we fell into bed together so easily?'

Colour touched her cheeks. 'I thought… I thought it was just me.'

'I assure you, it is mutual.' Zayed sat back in his chair. He felt surprisingly glad he'd told her, that he'd acknowledged what throbbed between them. It was a relief, like lancing a wound, relieving the pressure. The trouble was, what was he going to do about it now? Again he felt the flicker of pain at his temples.

'I'm…sorry,' Olivia said after a pause, sounding unsure. Zayed let out a laugh, trying not to wince in pain.

'This is not something you need to apologise for, Olivia.' He studied her, the colour in her face, the slight upturn of her lips. Had he pleased her by acknowledging what he felt for her? Did she find it so hard to believe? 'Have I given you another new experience, to have a man desire you so openly, so strongly?'

Her pupils flared. 'You have given me many new experiences, Prince Zayed.'

'I think we are past using my royal title.'

'Are we?' She gave a little shake of her head. 'I don't know where we are.'

And nor did he. But he knew where he wanted to be. He wanted to be in her arms, sinking himself inside her. The need throbbed inside him, obliterating every other consideration, overriding the pain growing inside his head.

She must have seen the heat in his eyes, because she let out a shaky laugh and looked down. 'Why me? I'm no one special. You must have had many women, Prince Zayed.'

'Not as many as you think.' A soldier's life in the desert had prohibited prolonged affairs. 'In fact, before you I had not been with a woman for many years.'

'Many years?' Her expression of astonishment was almost comical. Zayed smiled wryly.

'There has not been much opportunity.'

'That's why, then. You probably wouldn't look at me twice otherwise.'

'Why do you put yourself down?'

'I'm not.' She looked surprised. 'Just stating a truth.'

'It is not a truth to me.' Suddenly he felt the urge to show her how beautiful she was to him. How utterly lovely. 'Trust me on that, Olivia.' He held her gaze, willing her to see the desire in them. To feel it in herself.

And he knew she did; he heard it in the quickly indrawn breath, the way she touched her lips with her tongue. Neither of them moved.

Distantly, over the roar of his own heated blood, Zayed felt the pulse of pain in his eyes and spots danced before his eyes. Damn it, now was not the time for one of his migraines to torment him. Often he could simply will the pain away, but now Zayed feared it had gone too far.

Already his vision was blurring at the edges, the room going cloudy.

'Zayed…?' Olivia's voice was filled with alarm. 'Are you all right?'

So much for his seduction. Zayed tried for a laugh, but nearly retched instead. The pain came like a tidal wave now, drowning out everything else, waves thundering through his head. 'I…' He tried to speak but couldn't manage it.

'Are you in pain?' He felt Olivia's cool fingers on his cheek and breathed in her lemony scent. He closed his eyes, trying to block out the pain, but it was too late. Far too late.

'Headache,' he managed to get out through gritted teeth. Stupid of him to ignore the pain, to be so intent on seducing Olivia. If he'd gone to lie down in a dark room with a cool cloth on his head, he might have been able to avoid the worst of it. Now it would overtake him.

'A migraine,' she corrected softly. 'One of the Princesses gets them sometimes. They're terrible.'

'I just need to lie down.' He forced the words out, his teeth clenched so hard his jaw ached, cold sweat prickling on his back. He hated that Olivia was seeing him in such a weak and helpless way.

'Let me help you,' she said. 'Do you want me to call someone?'

'No.' He wanted to manage on his own, but he knew he couldn't. Still, better to keep the knowledge of his condition as closely guarded as possible. No one wanted to see their leader weak and in pain, and there was enough for his staff to worry about already.

'All right.' She placed one slender hand under his elbow. 'I'll help you to your bedroom.'

He rose unsteadily from his chair, leaning far more than he would have liked on Olivia's petite frame, yet she held his weight with surprising strength. She was slender and small, but she was not fragile. He felt the tensile strength running through her like a wire.

'It's not far,' he managed, and then stopped, because the spots dancing in his vision had coalesced into unending blackness. Standing there, Olivia's hand on his arm, her body bracing his, Zayed realised he could not see a thing. He was blind.

CHAPTER NINE

ZAYED STILLED AND Olivia sensed the shock in him, although at what she didn't know. Everything had spiralled out of control so rapidly—his admission of desire, the blatant invitation she'd seen in his eyes. If he hadn't developed a migraine, who knew what would have happened? Although Olivia could imagine it all too easily—and evocatively.

'What is it?' she asked because Zayed still hadn't moved.

'I...' His jaw bunched. 'I can't see.'

'Can't see? At all?'

'No.' The single word was a gasp of pain. A light sheen of sweat coated his pale face and his eyes were glazed.

'Let me get someone—'

'No.' The single word was like the snick of a blade. 'I don't want anyone else to see me like...this.'

'All right.' Olivia absorbed that, along with

his sudden blindness. Here, at least, she could be as useful as she knew how to be. As needed. 'Then we'd better get you to your bed.'

Slowly they walked from the room, Zayed gripping her hand tightly as she put her arm around him and guided him with halting steps.

'I don't actually know where your bedroom is,' she said in a low voice when they'd reached the thankfully empty hall outside the room where they'd been dining. 'Can you direct me?'

'Yes.' Zayed drew a quick breath. 'To the right, up the stairs, and then along the hallway.'

'All right.'

Each step felt painstakingly slow, as Zayed felt his way and battled his pain. Olivia could tell from his tightly clenched jaw just how much pain he was in, and her heart ached for him.

On the upstairs hallway Zayed suddenly went still, then shrugged away from her, even though Olivia could see that it cost him.

'What...?' she began in a whisper, but Zayed shook his head, a flinch of pain crossing his face.

Then his aide, Jahmal, came down the hallway. Zayed straightened.

'My Prince,' Jahmal said. He gave Olivia a cursory, curious glance and then looked away, dismissing her. 'Is everything well? I thought you were dining downstairs.'

'I'm finished.' Zayed spoke tersely. 'I will work in my room. I don't wish to be disturbed, please.'

Jahmal glanced at Olivia again, a frown marring his forehead. 'Very well…'

'Miss Taylor is helping me with a matter.'

Jahmal's frown cleared. 'The message to Sultan Hassan?'

'Yes. Leave us now, please.'

Jahmal sketched a short bow and strode down the hallway. After a few tense seconds Zayed expelled a low breath and then leaned against Olivia again; she took his weight, wrapping her arm around his waist.

'Get me to my room,' he said through clenched teeth. 'Before I humiliate myself even further.'

'There's no shame in pain.'

'You are wrong in that, at least for me.'

They didn't talk further; all their energy was expended on making it down the hallway.

'Here,' Zayed said when they were in front of an arched door that looked like any one of the dozen others along the corridor.

'How do you…?'

'I counted.'

Olivia turned the handle and the door swung open into a room that was sparsely furnished and masculine in every detail. She led him to the king-sized bed in the centre, and then guided him down onto the soft mattress. Zayed stretched out with a groan, one arm thrown over his eyes.

'Let me get you something,' Olivia suggested quietly. 'A damp cloth? Some tablets?'

'There's medicine in the bathroom.'

'All right.' She went into the sumptuous en suite, feeling as if she were invading his private space as she rifled through his medicine cabinet looking for the painkillers. She shook two out of the bottle and then poured a glass of water from the tap. She found a flannel and dampened it, and then brought it all back to Zayed.

'Here,' she said, perching on the edge of the bed. She pressed the tablets into his hand and then guided the glass of water to his lips. He swallowed in one powerful gulp and then subsided back onto the pillows. 'And this too,' Olivia said, and she gently laid the damp cloth across his forehead.

Zayed reached out his hand and found hers, lightly squeezing her fingers. 'Thank you.'

'I wish there was more I could do.'

'This has been more than I deserve.'

Deserve? It seemed an odd turn of phrase. 'Surely everyone deserves care when they're hurt?' Olivia said quietly.

'That depends,' Zayed murmured. Her hand

was still encased in his. Olivia watched his powerful chest rise and fall in steady breaths. Outside the sun was setting, sending streaks of light sliding across the floor, the sky lit up with the most vivid pinks and purples she'd ever seen. She wondered if she should go, if Zayed wanted to be left alone.

As if sensing her uncertainty, he squeezed her fingers again. 'Stay,' he entreated in a low voice. 'Stay with me.'

Something warm and wonderful unfurled in Olivia's heart, like a hug from the inside. She realised how much she'd wanted to stay, wanted him to want her to. 'Okay,' she said softly. 'Of course I will.'

She settled herself more comfortably against the pillows and Zayed drew her hand to his chest, still in his, so she could feel the thud of his heart against her palm.

His eyes were closed, dark, spiky lashes feathering the rugged planes of his cheeks. His mouth looked surprisingly lush and mobile on that harsh face, now softened as his breathing evened out. It could have been an hour or only a few minutes, but eventually Olivia realised he was asleep.

She'd lost track of time, of herself, in watching him, taking in every beautiful detail of his face and form, along with things she hadn't noticed before—a scar on his temple, another by his ear, both now faded to pale white streaks. Beneath his button-down shirt she could see the ridges of his chest and abdomen, perfectly and powerfully muscled.

She remembered how those muscles had felt under her questing hands, and she closed her eyes, trying to banish the memories for her own sanity, even though they were so achingly sweet. She'd never felt as treasured, as important, as she had in Zayed's embrace. Which was foolish, considering how she would most likely never see him again after the next day or two. The thought brought pain when Olivia knew it shouldn't, just as she knew every moment she spent in his company was dangerous because each one bound her closer and closer to this man—a man she would come to care for, if she let herself.

She told herself he was arrogant, assumptive and impatient. Yet she could understand why, considering how much he was fighting for. How much he'd lost. He'd barely mentioned the family whom had been murdered by Malouf, but Olivia sensed the deep, dark current of pain running right through his centre and it made her ache. He was also kind, considerate and gentle, and that made her ache even more.

She should leave, Olivia thought, before she

did something both dangerous and stupid and started to fall in love with him.

As quietly as she could she started to move from the bed, but the second she tried to slip her hand from his his grip tightened, and he hauled her forward so she was pressed against him. He moved again, seemingly in his sleep, so she was resting with her head on his shoulder, their hands still entwined on his chest. Once again his breathing evened out.

Olivia lay there, enjoying the feel of his powerful body pillowing her head, the steady thud of his heart under her cheek. She could smell his aftershave and feel his heat and it felt so very, very nice to lie here in Zayed's arms, the moon starting to rise, creating silver patterns on the floor. For a moment she let herself imagine having something like this every night—and the man in that far too pleasant fantasy was Zayed.

She wasn't falling in love with him. She absolutely couldn't be. And yet she longed. She couldn't deny the river of yearning that wound its way through her at this very moment, threatening to flood its banks as Zayed pulled her even closer, his other hand splayed possessively across her hip, his knee nudging in between her own.

Olivia closed her eyes, both savouring the sweetness of the moment and trying to fight its intensity. Because it would be so easy to let herself be swept away, let herself fall.

Eventually she started to relax and, with Zayed deeply asleep, she fell into a doze.

The pain in his head receded to a dull ache as Zayed drifted in and out of sleep, conscious of the softness of the bed and the even more enticing softness of the warm, pliant body next to his. Sleep still fogged his mind as he pulled the body closer, enjoying the way her breasts were pressed against his chest, her hips nudging his. Heat flared, and when she arched a little bit against him, it flared hotter and brighter.

In one smooth movement he rolled on top of her, his hands seeking and finding all the soft curves and tempting dips of her body. He slid his hand up one slender, perfect thigh to the warmth at her centre, and she moaned. The heat inside him was a pulsing need, taking over all his senses.

He pressed his knee between hers, nudging her legs apart even further, positioning his body so he could bury himself in her welcoming depths.

She arched up to meet him and Zayed braced himself on his forearms. The pain in his head flickered, a second's distraction that had him suddenly stilling. God in heaven, what was he doing? He could jeopardise everything by making love with Olivia now.

With a groan he rolled off her, his body aching, his heart thudding. It felt like the hardest thing he'd ever done.

After a taut second Olivia rolled the other way, curling her knees up to her chest. The pain thudded through Zayed's head again and he closed his eyes.

'Olivia…'

'It's all right.' Her voice was a broken whisper, a ragged breath.

'I'm sorry.'

'I know.'

'The moment… I was asleep…' He felt that nothing he said could help. 'I got carried away and I shouldn't have.'

'I got carried away too.' She spoke softly, her back to him. When he cracked an eye open he could see the tender nape of her neck, and it made guilt rush through him all over again. Enough with the guilt. He needed to get Olivia out of his life, or he needed to get out of hers, and the sooner the better. He couldn't let himself get distracted. Duty was far more important. He closed his eyes again and pictured the helicopter filled with flames. Imagined he could see his father's and brother's faces, although he hadn't been able to at the time. And then he saw himself running away, hustled by his staff to safety. Even now, ten years later, the shame of it bit deep. *Coward.* No one had ever said it to him, but he'd felt it. How he'd felt it.

'Survivor's guilt,' his advisors had told him more than once. *It happens.* And he knew, in his head, in his gut, that he'd needed to survive. He was the last of the line, the only one remaining of a dynasty that stretched back centuries, the only person who could wrest control from Malouf. But in his heart he felt the guilt, the shame, and he didn't think it would ever leave him.

Which was why he had to focus on his duty and how to atone for the past. And the only service Olivia Taylor could provide for him was going away quietly.

As if she read his thoughts, she rose from the bed in one fluid movement, shrugging off the hand he hadn't even realised he'd stretched out to her.

'I'll go,' she said quietly, smoothing her dress down and slipping on her heels. 'You need your sleep. Is the headache better?'

'A bit.'

'Good.' She gave him a fleeting smile that didn't meet her eyes.

'Thank you, Olivia. I am sorry.'

'It's fine.' She lifted her chin. 'It's fine,' she said again, and then she was gone.

The silence of the room felt endless and empty as Zayed lay on his bed, his head aching as much as his heart. He didn't care about Olivia, he told himself. He didn't care about anyone like that and never would. Caring was inviting vulnerability and pain, something he had no intention of doing. If you cared about someone, your enemies could and would use it against you. He would never allow that to happen again.

But he still felt guilty and restless, wishing things had been different. If he'd kidnapped the right woman…*then he would never have met Olivia.*

The very fact that he could think that showed him how quickly and decisively he needed to act. Tomorrow he would send the message to Sultan Hassan and make sure Olivia wrote her letter. He would set the wheels in motion for all this to be repaired.

By the time Zayed fell asleep, the pale pink streaks of dawn were lighting the sky and he didn't waken until after the noon hour. Thankfully his headache was gone, and after showering and dressing he went in search of Jahmal and then Olivia.

'Has there been any news on the Sultan?' he asked Jahmal as they sat in his office in the west wing of the palace, the arched windows open to the sky.

'Only that he is displeased,' Jahmal answered with a grimace. 'Queen Aliya has taken Princess Halina to Italy,' he added. 'To keep her from being kidnapped.'

'As if I would try the same thing twice.' Zayed rubbed his temples. 'It was a foolish plan in the first place, even if it felt necessary at the time.'

'He still might be open to a communication from you,' Jahmal offered.

'He'd better be,' Zayed returned grimly. 'I'll send a gift with the message—some of my finest Arabians.'

'The Sultan is known for his love of horses.'

'Yes.' Briefly Zayed thought about how Olivia had said she couldn't ride. Right then he should have known it wasn't the Princess. Why had he been so unbelievably blind, seeing only what he'd wanted to see?

'I need to find Miss Taylor,' he said. 'Do you know where she is?'

'She has spent the morning with some of the women,' Jahmal answered. 'In the gardens.'

Some of his staff and soldiers had wives who lived in the palace. It was an isolated but safe existence, and he knew they all longed for the day when they could return to Arjah and their normal lives. They'd all been waiting a long time for that.

Outside the sun was shining brightly, the air still holding a hint of crispness from the cold night. Zayed strolled through the gardens, enjoying the sunlight on his face. He'd forgotten how pleasant it was out here, with the orange and lemon trees, the trailing flowers, the tinkle of the many fountains.

He wandered for several minutes through various landscaped gardens, each one surrounded by its own hedge, until he came onto a small, pretty courtyard with a fountain splashing in the middle and several ornate benches around. Lahela, one of his aides' wives who had just had a baby, was laughing at something Olivia said.

And Olivia... She sat on a bench, wearing a casual sundress the exact shade of her eyes, her hair falling down her back in tumbling chestnut waves, Lahela's baby on her lap gurgling up at her. She looked so happy and natural, almost as if...

Zayed's mind suddenly screeched to a halt, freezing on one simple fact that he'd completely ignored since he'd first taken Olivia and married her. Had slept with her.

He hadn't used birth control.

Of course he hadn't. It had been his wedding night; if he'd got Halina pregnant it simply would have strengthened his cause. Since then he hadn't thought for a moment, a single second, that Olivia could be pregnant...pregnant with his child. His heir.

Her laughter drifted across the courtyard, a deep, delighted sound, and she bounced the fat, smiling baby on her knee. Then she looked up and her gaze caught Zayed's, clashing with it so he felt as if he'd come up against a brick wall.

Her eyes widened, pupils flaring, and colour touched her cheeks. She looked away, bending her head so her hair fell forward and hid her face. Zayed's chest tightened. The pain he thought he'd banished crept back.

Keeping his voice as even as he could, he greeted the other women in the courtyard before turning his attention resolutely to Olivia. She still wasn't looking at him.

'Miss Taylor,' he said. 'May I have a word?'

Olivia handed the baby back to Lahela, trying not to let her trepidation show. Her heart was thumping in her chest as she followed Zayed out of the garden, both of them silent. He seemed angry, and she could only suppose it was about last night...and what had almost happened between them.

She'd spent most of the night practically writhing in shame—and unsated desire. When Zayed had started touching her, she'd been helpless to do anything but respond. Want. Beg. Just as he'd once said. Even now the memory made her face flood with colour and she closed her eyes briefly against it. How could she be so helpless when it came to her response to this man?

Zayed walked swiftly through several corridors and then finally opened the door to a small, ornate room that looked like a private study. Olivia stood in the centre of the room, knotting her hands together so they wouldn't shake.

Zayed closed the door and then whirled around to face her. 'Could you be pregnant?' he demanded tersely.

Olivia blinked. That had not been what she was expecting at all. 'Pregnant…?'

'From our wedding night.' He ground the words out, his mouth compressing. 'I did not use birth control and, as you were a virgin, I question whether you were on it.'

'I'm not,' she confirmed quietly.

'And you have no…issues with fertility?'

Her face burned even hotter. 'None that I know of, no.'

Zayed swore under his breath and turned away from her in one abrupt movement. At least she knew how he felt about a possible pregnancy, and could she even be surprised? He was planning to divorce her. Of course he didn't want her to have his baby. Yet strangely, stupidly, Olivia felt hurt.

Zayed squared his shoulders, his taut back

to her. 'So there is a chance you could be pregnant?'

'Yes, I suppose.'

He turned around. 'You suppose?'

Irritation bit. 'Yes, I suppose. I'm not omniscient, Zayed, and this is not my fault.' Her voice quavered. 'I thought you'd realised that, but it seems you're back to blaming me.'

'No, I'm sorry.' He rubbed a hand wearily over his face. 'I don't mean to blame you. I blame myself, if anyone, for being so presumptuous and rash. It's just another complication in what is already a very complicated situation. And I should have thought of it sooner.' He dropped his hand from his face, giving her a surprisingly wry and honest look. 'I'm ashamed that I did not.'

'It's understandable,' Olivia murmured. Her flush had thankfully faded but she still felt embarrassed to be talking about this at all. 'You've had a lot on your mind.'

'Yes, but…' He stared at her for a moment, his gaze hard and assessing. Olivia looked back at him warily. 'You realised,' he said, and it was a statement. 'A while ago, I think. Yet you didn't say anything.'

'What was I supposed to say?'

'That you might be pregnant?' His brows drew together in a line. 'I know it's stating the obvious, but it is clearly a potential issue, and one that we needed to discuss.'

'I suppose I didn't see the point of discussing it until it was a certainty.'

'But by that point you might have been out of my life!' Zayed took a step closer to her. 'Were you considering not telling me about my child, Olivia?'

She gazed at him in disbelief. 'Are you serious, Zayed? Are you accusing me of something that hasn't even happened yet? I may not even be pregnant. I'm probably not.'

'Probably? Why do you say that?'

She shrugged. 'I don't know, but there's a good chance I'm not.'

'But there is a chance you are. That is the point.' He gave her a long, level look. 'Would you not have told me?'

'I... I don't know. I didn't think that far ahead.' She turned away from him, hating this whole conversation, all the what-ifs that had come into her life when everything had once been so certain, so safe, if a little staid. And she hated that a conversation about their possible child was so clinical, so cold. Some part of her wished for an alternative scenario, one where they hoped for such a thing. Revelled in the miracle of it. Was she insane?

'What did you think, then?' Zayed asked.

'Why does it matter?' she demanded, whirling around again. 'Why do you always have to make me feel guilty, Zayed?'

Remorse crumpled his features for a split second. 'Is that how I always make you feel?' he asked in a low voice, and Olivia heard the sudden innuendo in it, as well as the intent.

'No, but now... I know this is a potential problem, Zayed, but it's not my fault.'

'I know it isn't.' He closed his eyes and shook his head. 'I'm sorry. I don't mean to act in such a way. When I'm around you...' He stopped, and curiosity flickered through her, along with an excitement she could hardly credit.

'When you're around me...?' she prompted.

Zayed opened his eyes and the blazing heat she saw in their depths lit a fire in her soul. 'When I'm around you I lose my head. My very self. I can think of nothing but you...of having you.'

Excitement exploded inside her; she felt dizzy with it. Dizzy with desire, the rush of it so unexpected considering they'd just been arguing. But had it ever really gone away? She'd been fighting it, in one form or another, since the moment she'd met him.

'I know it's wrong,' Zayed murmured. 'I know it's foolish. I know we shouldn't, and yet I want to. I crave you, Olivia. Why do I crave you so much?'

'I crave you,' Olivia whispered. She couldn't look away from his fierce face, every muscle straining as he sought to control himself. Then he couldn't, and as she watched in breathless anticipation he swallowed the space between them in a couple of strides and she was in his arms, his mouth coming down hard and demanding on hers, the dam they'd both been constructing finally broken, the desire rushing in.

His mouth was hard and soft, the kiss sweet and strong at the same time, both sexy and sacred. *Wonderful.* Olivia returned the kiss with all that she had, unable to stop from giving him her everything. Zayed backed her across the room and her bottom came up against a desk. He growled against her mouth as he hoisted her on top of it, papers and books spilling onto the floor with a clatter.

No sweet seduction now; the force of their desire swept them along, caught up in its tidal wave as it dragged them under. Zayed nudged her legs apart with his own and then stood between her thighs as he plundered her mouth, his hands roving possessively over her body, demanding even more from her. And she gave it. Her mind a frenzied blur of sensation, she gave it willingly, joyfully, because, no matter how impossible their situation was, this man called to something in her that she hadn't even known she had—and she called to him. That alone was a miracle, a wonderful, incredible miracle.

She felt Zayed's fingers on the edge of her underwear, pulling it down. She moaned aloud, squirming against the feel of his hand, unable to wait even a second longer for the satiation they both craved, needing it with every fibre of their beings. This. Again *this*.

Zayed fumbled with his trousers, and with one swift stroke he was inside her. Olivia's muscles clenched around him and she wrapped her legs around his waist, uniting their bodies as closely and completely as she could, glorying in the feeling of it, the pleasure as well as the unity. She felt complete again, as if everything in her had been waiting to feel this way since the last time.

Zayed began to move, each strong, sure stroke sending Olivia higher to that dizzying peak. She matched his movements, learning the rhythm, finding it naturally, as if this had always been a part of her. As if he had.

And then she reached that glittering pinnacle, a cry bursting from her like a song of joy. She buried her head against Zayed's shoulder as the spasms of pleasure shuddered through her body before receding in a lazy tide, leaving her feeling boneless and sated.

Seconds and then minutes ticked by, slowly,

and then ominously. Dimly Olivia realised they'd just had unprotected sex again. And, if she wasn't already pregnant, she could be now.

Another few seconds ticked by, each one tenser than the last, then Zayed withdrew from her, cleaning himself up quickly before adjusting his trousers. His face looked as if it had been hewn from stone, his eyes dark and fathomless.

Olivia pulled her sundress down over her hips, smoothing the crumpled material, unable to look him in the eye. The wonderful, lazy feeling of sated desire was leaving her and only trepidation remained. *What now?*

'It seems,' Zayed said in a tight voice, 'I cannot control myself around you.'

Olivia moistened her lips with her tongue. 'I'm sorry.'

'*You're* sorry? I am the one who should be sorry. I am the one who should be thinking of my kingdom, my people, my duty.' His voice broke and he whirled away from her, scrubbing his eyes with the heels of his hands as if he could obliterate the memory of what they'd just done.

With a jolt Olivia realised how much of Zayed's anger was directed at himself, rooted in guilt. He'd hinted as much, but she hadn't really believed it. Now she saw a depth of pain in the tense lines of his body, in the torment so clearly written on his face.

'Zayed,' she whispered, a plea, although for what she could not say. She just wanted to offer him comfort, even though she feared she had none to give him. None he would take, except what he already had, and now they were both living with the aftermath of regret.

'You have no idea,' Zayed said in a low voice of anguish. 'No idea—and how could you? No idea of what is at stake.'

'I know your marriage to Princess Halina is very important,' Olivia offered, wanting to show him she understood. Even now, she understood.

'Important?' Zayed choked out the word. 'It isn't *important*. It's essential. To finally have a political leader publicly recognise and fight for my rightful claim…' He closed his eyes. 'But it's not even that. It's what I see every night before I go to sleep. Every time I close my eyes.'

Olivia drew a short, shocked breath. 'What did you see, Zayed?' she asked softly. 'Tell me what you see.'

Zayed knew he shouldn't say anything more. He shouldn't tell her anything. Heaven knew, he'd told her enough, done enough, already. Even now the aftershocks of their explosive lovemaking were rippling through him, reminding him how sizzlingly potent their attraction was. It frightened him, the intensity of what he felt. When she was near him it was as if he was swallowed up by a vortex of need. He forgot everything.

'Zayed.' Olivia touched his arm, her fingers as light as the wings of a butterfly. 'Please. Tell me what haunts you so much.'

He resisted, because to tell was to admit his weakness, his shame. He didn't talk of the loss of his family to anyone. Everyone knew the facts, of course; it was a matter of national history. But no one knew about his nightmares, his helplessness. Yet some contrary, shameful part of him wanted to tell Olivia. Wanted to share the burden which, considering everything he'd already put her through, seemed more than unfair.

'Tell me.' Her voice was soft, a soothing balm to his fractured spirit. Her fingers stroked his arm.

Zayed let out a shuddering sigh. 'I see my father and older brother in the helicopter. Going down. I always see them.'

'Oh, Zayed.' Olivia gave a sorrowful little gasp. 'Of course. I'm so sorry.'

She knew the facts, he realised, just as everyone else did. The bare facts—the bomb that had exploded in the helicopter, the attempt on his mother's life, his cowardly scurry to freedom. Not that anyone would say so to his face, but he knew. He knew.

'I didn't realise you'd seen it,' Olivia said quietly after a moment, her hand still on his arm, as if she could imbue him with the strength he was just beginning to realise she had. The incredible strength. 'I didn't think you were there.'

'I was. I was in the palace, watching them take off. My father and his heir.' His lips twisted. They'd been going to do their civic duty, to speak at the opening of a hospital in another city, a landmark of Kalidar's recent transition to national healthcare. Of course Malouf had taken that away. He'd taken away so much. 'Perhaps you're wondering why I didn't go with them,' he said, his voice harsh, his breathing ragged. Olivia's fingers tensed on his arm.

'No,' she said carefully. 'But perhaps you want to tell me?'

He didn't, but he would, because she deserved to know. After everything, he owed her that much. The truth he'd kept from everyone else. 'I was bored by the idea,' he said flatly. 'I'd just got back from Cambridge and I found the desert so very tedious. My father asked me to accompany them and I said no. Minutes later I watched them go down in flames.'

Olivia was silent for a moment. 'Then perhaps you should be thankful,' she said finally, 'that you were so bored.'

He drew back from her, disgusted by the suggestion. Just as he was disgusted by his own actions all those years ago. 'Thankful?' he repeated, the word a sneer. 'How can I be? I deserved to die that day!'

'And if you had Kalidar would have no rightful King.'

'Don't you think I know that?' He felt caught between fury and despair. 'Why do you think I fight so hard? Why did I try to kidnap the Princess?' He let out a harsh bark of laughter. 'Everything I do, everything, is for their memory. And for mine. Because I failed my family once, and I never will again.'

'I understand why you are so driven,' Olivia said steadily. 'But you did not plant that bomb in the helicopter, Zayed. You did not poison your mother.'

She knew that too, then. 'She died in my arms a few months later. Wasted away to nothing. But the doctors didn't even think it was the poison. She'd recovered from that. It was from grief. She had no reason to live.' He felt a spasm of pain, like a knife thrust in his gut. For a second he couldn't breathe, and he swung away from Olivia, hating that she could see this weakness exposed in him. See his need, his hurt.

'I'm sorry,' Olivia said quietly. 'I know how painful that must have been for you.'

Something in her voice made him ask, 'You do?'

Olivia was silent for a moment. 'My mother

died when I was young. Cancer—very quick.
I don't remember much about her, but we have
photos—family photos that are so different
from what I became used to as a child. Looking at them is like seeing someone else's life.'

Zayed frowned, waiting for her to go on.
'After she died, my father shut down. He hired
a nanny and hardly ever saw me, and then sent
me to boarding school as soon as he could. He
was a stranger to me but, when I see those photos, I realise he wasn't always that way. Before
my mother died, he hugged me and tickled me
and read me stories at night. I have the photo-
graphic proof.' Her voice was wistful and sad.
'And it made me realise that he *chose* to be
a stranger. He didn't think I was worth being
something more.'

'Perhaps he couldn't be anything more, because of grief.'

'Perhaps,' she acknowledged, 'and perhaps
your mother didn't have the strength to go on
just for you. But it still hurts. It still feels like
you failed somehow. Like you weren't enough.'

Her perception left him breathless, because
he knew she was exactly right. His mother's
death, the way she'd seemed to choose it over
life, had been a further blow after his father and
brother's death. A further and harder grief, because they could have held each other up, sup-

ported each other, been strong for each other. And she'd chosen for him to go it alone.

'I'm sorry, Zayed.' Olivia stepped closer to him, reaching up on her tiptoes to cup his cheek with her palm. Zayed closed his eyes. 'I'm so sorry.'

'You have nothing to be sorry for, Olivia,' he said. 'I know that absolutely.'

'I'm sorry all the same. For all you've endured, and for so long. I'm in awe of your strength. To keep fighting for all these years, to be so determined; I wish I possessed such courage. Such conviction.'

'You are brave,' Zayed told her, opening his eyes and giving her a small smile. 'You have shown me that.'

'Brave?' Olivia shrugged. 'I don't think so. But I try to be useful. That's something, at least.'

Useful? It sounded like so little. Did Olivia hope for more from her life? For the love of a husband, of children? She wouldn't get it from him, and yet...

'I promise I will do everything in my power to make your marriage with Princess Halina go forward,' she told him. 'I'll write that letter, whatever it takes.'

The letter, the damned letter. Zayed stared at her, a conviction growing inside him, crystallising into clarity. 'No,' he said, and Olivia's eyes widened in surprise. 'I don't want you to write a letter. I don't want to contact the Sultan, not until we know whether you're pregnant or not.'

'But...'

'And, considering what we just did, we may have to wait awhile.'

'You can't jeopardise your country's future—'

'I already have. Kidnapping you has infuriated Hassan. He's taken Halina to Italy, away from my possible clutches.' He smiled wryly. 'Not that I would try such a foolhardy and desperate act again.'

'But you will contact him? You will try to make amends?'

How could he, when he already had a wife, and one who could very well be pregnant? Zayed shook his head. 'Like I said, not until we have ascertained your condition.'

Olivia's hand crept to her belly in a gesture as old as time. 'And if I am pregnant?' she asked.

'Then,' Zayed said, his tone brooking no argument whatsoever, 'we stay married. The child in your belly will be my heir and the future King of Kalidar.'

CHAPTER TEN

OLIVIA GAZED OUT at the mountain peaks dusted with snow, at the sun shining brilliantly, and let out a sigh that was half happy, half discontented. They'd been in Rubyhan for nearly two weeks now and it had been a surprisingly wonderful two weeks.

Olivia, as she was wont to do, had made herself useful helping out in the administrative office—as her knowledge of both French and Italian had proved useful—and also taking care of Lahela's baby so the new mother could get an occasional rest. The atmosphere in the palace was a surprisingly cheerful one, with everyone determined to work towards the same important goal. Zayed had an incredibly loyal team, and they believed in him utterly.

Which made Olivia understand why he was so private with them. He didn't share his headaches or his nightmares or any of his worries or concerns, as far as Olivia could see. He presented himself as a fortress, solid and impenetrable, because everyone was depending on him. It was, Olivia suspected, a heavy burden to bear. And it made her feel more honoured that he'd shared those things with her. As impossible as it seemed, they did have a connection, one that grew deeper on her side every day. One she could no longer deny, at least to herself.

Over the last few weeks Zayed had taken time out of his busy days and spent it with her, and they'd shared several meals as well as a few sunny afternoons simply whiling away the hours and getting to know each other.

Olivia had treasured those stolen hours, the easy conversation, the glimpses of humour, the attraction that always, always simmered between them. She'd started to feel comfortable with him, known by him, and that made her desire and care for him all the more. Which was foolhardy in the extreme, because she knew it was all likely to come to an end when she found out she wasn't pregnant.

And if she was pregnant and Zayed kept her as his Queen? That was the possibility that brought her to both the heights of hope and the depths of fear. The more time she spent with him—the more time she saw his solicitude, his moments of humour, his care for his people and even for her—she feared she was falling in love with him. And that was something that she couldn't allow to happen. Not when she knew a marriage to Zayed would only happen for expediency's sake, not because of love. And she didn't know if that was something she could accept, not in the long term. But in any case, she might not even have a choice. If she was pregnant, Zayed would not let her walk away. And Olivia had no idea how she felt about that.

A knock sounded at the door of her bedroom, and Olivia turned from the stunning view. 'Hello?' she called in Arabic. 'Come in.'

'It's me.' Zayed appeared around the door, looking crisply attractive in a western-style business suit. When not among the tribes of the desert, he tended to wear western clothes, a preference he'd said was from his Cambridge days. Olivia had enjoyed getting to know this little detail about him, as well as countless others. He preferred coffee rather than tea, and he listened to jazz. He had glasses for reading, and a partiality for Agatha Christie, something that had made her smile.

'Hi,' she said now, trying to ignore the tumble of her heart simply at the sight of him. 'How are you?'

'Oh, fine.' He braced one shoulder against the doorway, surveying her bedroom with a distracted yet strangely purposeful air. Olivia wondered what he wanted. Although he'd made a point of seeing her every day, he'd never come to her bedroom first thing in the morning. She felt a little frisson of fear. Was this odd sort of honeymoon period over already?

'It's been two weeks,' Zayed said, and there was an intractable note in his voice. Olivia stilled, one hand resting on the stone window-sill.

'Yes,' she agreed cautiously. 'Thirteen days, to be exact.'

His agate gaze searched hers. 'You should take a pregnancy test tomorrow, then.'

'Is there one available?' Olivia asked as lightly as she could. Her heart had started to hammer just at the thought of taking such a test. And, as luxurious as their accommodation was, they were in the middle of nowhere. How would Zayed procure a pregnancy test?

'I'm having it flown in.'

She swallowed. 'Oh.'

'Better to know than not.'

Which sounded rather awful, and she couldn't tell anything from his expression. 'Yes, I suppose.'

So as soon as tomorrow this could all be over. He'd send her away and reopen negotiations with Sultan Hassan for Halina. Why, oh, why, did that thought have to hurt so much?

'I'm having dinner with a government official from France tonight,' Zayed said abruptly. Olivia looked at him in surprise.

'Here?'

'He's flying in.'

'Along with the pregnancy test?' she couldn't help but quip, and Zayed gave her a tight smile. 'On the same helicopter, as it happens, although obviously two very separate requests. I thought you could join us for dinner.'

'You—what?' Now she was really flummoxed. Although she'd enjoyed her time at Rubyhan, and had socialised and interacted with just about everyone there, she still felt as if she were being hidden away from the rest of the world, Zayed's unfortunate mistake, his dirty little secret. She'd hardly expected to be introduced to someone important, someone who expected Zayed to be married to Princess Halina and not a governess nobody.

'You speak French,' Zayed pointed out. 'You told me a few days ago.'

'Yes, but...'

'And having you there will make the dinner less formal, which is important at this stage.'

'This stage of what?'

'France might be willing to support me against Malouf,' Zayed explained. 'This is their initial approach.'

'Okay.' She didn't understand the ins and outs of the politics, but she accepted that Zayed did, and if he wanted her there, she would go. 'How…how are you going to introduce me?'

'Simply as my companion. I do not think Pierre Serrat will ask any awkward questions. He is a diplomat, after all.'

Olivia nodded, unsure how she felt about any of this. It was so unexpected, yet the last few weeks had been filled with unexpected things.

They'd been exciting, she acknowledged, and she'd known more happiness here than she ever had in the Sultan's palace, a fact which made her feel a little sad. When and if Zayed sent her away, she would do something different with her life, she vowed. She would go to Paris, get a job, live independently as she never had before. The prospect made her wilt inside. She was falling in love with him, she acknowledged despondently. With every moment, every second she spent in his company, she tumbled a little bit further. And there was nothing she could do about it.

'I'll send Anna to you later,' Zayed said. 'To prepare for tonight.' Olivia nodded, and he paused in the doorway. 'Thank you, Olivia.'

'You're welcome.' The words were squeezed out. Zayed nodded once, then he was gone. She stared at the empty doorway for a moment, wishing she knew what was in his head. Was he hoping that she wasn't pregnant, so he could get rid of her as soon as possible?

Of course he is, you ninny.

No matter how pleasant the last two weeks had been, and they'd been very pleasant for her, Zayed was a man on a mission, one he'd explained to her himself, one she understood and sympathised with. He needed Sultan Hassan's cooperation too much to jeopardise it by staying married to her.

She was so foolish, half daring to dream about a life with a baby and a husband at her side. A man, she reminded herself ruthlessly, who would be there only by duty, not by desire. Far better for her as well as for Zayed if she hadn't fallen pregnant. She knew that, even if in her weaker moments she didn't feel it.

Olivia spent the morning as she had intended to, proofreading some correspondence in French. It was wordy stuff, about support for Kalidar's social programmes, and made Olivia wonder about Serrat's visit. What exactly were he and Zayed going to talk about? And why did Zayed want her there?

Anna fetched her in the afternoon and Olivia looked in surprise at her bedroom which, it seemed, had been transformed into a beauty spa.

'Prince Zayed thought you would enjoy some spa treatments,' Anna said with a smile.

Olivia spent the next few hours being pampered and massaged, tweezed and trimmed. When she finally emerged from the bathroom in a huge terry-cloth robe, she felt as if she were glowing from the inside.

Anna had laid out an evening gown, a column of deep blue, with a diamanté belt and detailing on the hem. Diamanté-studded high heels matched the outfit. It was the most gorgeous dress Olivia had ever seen.

Anna helped her slip it on and zipped up the back, then one of the beauty stylists came to do her hair in a loose chignon, a few dark tendrils slipping down artfully to frame her face.

'I feel like Cinderella,' Olivia said with a little laugh, but inside she felt a pulse of both disappointment and longing. She needed to give herself the reminder, because she *was* Cinderella. It was going to turn midnight on her very soon…if she wasn't pregnant.

And if she was…

'Come,' Anna said as she handed her a matching gauzy wrap. 'Prince Zayed and Monsieur Serrat are both waiting.'

With her heart starting to thud in anticipation, Olivia followed Anna from the bedroom to a small, private salon on the ground floor, its arched windows overlooking the back gardens that had been developed on the mountainside, surprisingly lush and green.

'Ah, here she is.' Zayed turned as she entered the candlelit room, giving her a smile that was both reassuring and devastating. He wore black tie, and the crisp white shirt and midnight tuxedo jacket suited him perfectly, the ultimate foil to his bronzed skin and ebony hair. Olivia became breathless just looking at him. 'Monsieur Serrat, please let me introduce Miss Olivia Taylor.'

Olivia turned to the second man, who looked to be in his forties, with thinning hair and a kind smile as he nodded at her. 'Pleased to meet you, *mademoiselle*.'

'And you, *monsieur*,' Olivia answered in French. 'It is a pleasure.'

Pierre Serrat's face lit up. 'You speak French.'

'Mais bien sûr,' Olivia answered with a laugh. She came further into the room, her dress swishing about her ankles. She felt so beautiful in this dress, beautiful and confident in a way she never had before. She extended her hand, and with a grin Pierre Serrat kissed it. Olivia glanced at Zayed and saw a flash of something turn his eyes silver—admiration and perhaps even pride. An answering emotion fired through her, buoying her confidence all the more.

It wasn't just the dress that made her feel this way. It was Zayed. Knowing that he'd needed her, that he wanted her here at his side…it felt like the ultimate empowerment.

The member of staff who was quietly serving them handed Olivia a glass of champagne, and the conversation flowed easily, from where Olivia had learned her French to the places she'd visited in France.

'And what do you think of Kalidar?' Serrat asked as they were seated at a small, intimate table laid for three. 'It is quite different from Europe.'

'I've been living in Abkar for several years,' Olivia replied. 'So I am used to this part of the world. And I find Kalidar to be quite beautiful, even if it is a harsh beauty.'

'Well said,' Serrat answered, raising his glass, and Olivia tilted her head in acknowledgement.

The conversation continued through five courses of a meal that could have been served in a Michelin-starred restaurant in Paris and, as Zayed had promised, Serrat did not ask any awkward questions about who she was or what she was doing there. Neither did he talk of politics or policy. Olivia suspected that would come later, when she wasn't present, if it hadn't already happened.

As she sipped her wine she let herself drift

into a daydream that this was her reality—that Zayed had been restored as King and she was his Queen. That they were entertaining together, as they often would, a partnership, a team. It was such a pleasant daydream, but it also created an ache in her that was painful. It hurt to let herself imagine things that would never come to pass. Even if Zayed insisted on keeping her as his Queen, she knew instinctively that he would not want the kind of loving partnership she dreamed of. But perhaps it would come in time...

Was it foolishness to hope for such a thing? Madness? Yet she did. To her own weakness and shame, she did, because she wanted to be pregnant with Zayed's child so she could live as his Queen...whatever he felt for her.

Olivia sparkled like the most brilliant jewel. All evening Zayed had trouble keeping his eyes off her and so, he'd noticed bemusedly, did Serrat. He'd made the right decision in having Olivia attend. Serrat had relaxed, seeing the western influence in Zayed's life, speaking his own language. Their discussions that afternoon had been tenuous and wary; France was willing to support Zayed against Malouf but wanted to be reassured that Zayed would take Kalidar in a different direction—and what better way to prove that than by taking a western wife?

When Jahmal had told him that Sultan Hassan had sent Halina away and was refusing to accept his message or his gifts, Zayed had realised he needed to think seriously about an alternative. And he had, quite suddenly, realised that Olivia *was* the alternative, and a good one at that…even if she wasn't pregnant.

Admittedly, he would have preferred a wife with further-reaching connections, but Olivia's background as a diplomat's daughter, her ease with languages and the fact that she was European were all points in her favour. If she was carrying his child, so much the better.

It was after midnight when Serrat said goodnight, and left Zayed and Olivia alone in the dining room, the room flickering with shadows and candlelight. Zayed ached just to look at her, her slender body encased in the sheath-like evening gown, the diamanté details making her sparkle so she looked like a blue flame.

'You were lovely tonight,' he said in a low voice. 'Perfect.'

'I didn't do much,' Olivia answered with a little laugh. 'Just made small talk.'

'Which was exactly what was needed.' Zayed had a desperate urge to make love to her. He'd been fighting it all evening; he hadn't touched her in ten days, since that madness had over-taken them both in his study, and he'd had her on his own desk. Even now he couldn't believe how quickly and completely he'd lost control, yet it had felt so good. So right. He didn't think he'd ever tire of her—and why should he? She was his wife. And she could stay his wife.

'Do you think France will support your claim?' Olivia asked. Her eyes were wide as she looked at him and Zayed knew she felt it too. The desire twanged between them; the air felt electric. He reached forward and took her hand, her fingertips sliding along his.

'I hope so. Serrat will return to his govern-ment with a very favourable report, I have no doubt, and in no small part thanks to you.' He drew her towards him and she came hesitantly, a question in her eyes. 'I want to make love to you, Olivia,' Zayed said, a ragged note entering his voice. His need was too great to hide it. 'I've been wanting to make love to you all evening. For ten days, in fact. I'm in agony.'

She laughed softly at that, and as her hips nudged his heat flared. 'I would hate to be the cause of your pain.'

'You are the only one who can assuage it.' His hands cupped her face, his palms sliding over her silken skin. He could never get enough of her. She tilted her face up to gaze at him, everything about her open and trusting. When he told her he intended to keep her as his Queen no matter what, pregnancy or no, she would give no objections. Of that he was certain.

Zayed lowered his head and brushed his lips against Olivia's. She tasted cool and sweet and so very lovely. He deepened the kiss, loving the feel of her softness against the hard planes of his chest and thighs.

'Zayed,' she murmured against his mouth, a protest. He stilled, surprised. Surely she would not deny him now? She wanted this as much as he did—even more. 'Someone will come in.' She gestured to the table strewn with dirty dishes. 'To clear up.'

'Not while I'm in here,' Zayed answered confidently, and started drawing her towards him again, aching to feel her mouth once more.

Olivia shook her head. 'They'll be waiting until you leave. And they'll be tired, having served us all night. Let's not make them wait any longer.'

'You are thinking of my staff?'

Olivia's eyes flashed. 'Having worked in a royal household for four years, I have some sympathy.'

'Of course.' With a smile he reached for her hand. 'You are talking sense, especially as I would much rather make love to you on a bed. My bed.'

Her cheeks went pink. 'Do you really think this is a—'

'I don't think.' Zayed cut her off before she could verbalise any concerns. 'I know. I want you, Olivia, and you want me. It's that simple.'

'Yes, but...' Shadows crept into her stormy eyes. 'What about...?'

'Shh.' He silenced her with a kiss. 'Tonight is for us. Only for us.' And, as she kissed him back, he knew he had her acquiescence. Her surrender.

Silently, holding her hand, he led her to his bedroom. The corridors were dark and shadowy, the mood singing with expectation. Her hand felt small and fragile in his.

Back in his bedroom his bed had been turned down by one his staff, the lamps turned to low, the perfect setting for seduction. Except this wasn't even a seduction; this was both of them wanting each other. Revelling in each other.

As soon as the door closed behind them Zayed turned to Olivia and she came willingly; their bodies clashed, their mouths tangled and his blood and heart both sang. He backed her towards the bed and she tripped on her dress; the fragile material tore but Zayed didn't care. He didn't care about anything but the woman in his arms.

A single tug of the zip and the torn garment slithered off her, leaving her in nothing but a sheer bra and pants. She shivered slightly and Zayed realised she was nervous. The last time they'd been together, it had been rushed and urgent, and the time before that it had been a consummation, a matter of expediency. Tonight felt different for both of them.

'You're beautiful,' he said softly as he smoothed his hand from her shoulder to her hip. 'Utterly beautiful.'

Relief flashed across her face and then, with an impish smile, she reached for the studs on his shirt. Her fingers trembled slightly as she undid the first one but then, emboldened by the throaty growl he couldn't help but give, she undid the others, the studs clattering to the ground, then pushed his shirt aside before resting her palms flat on his chest.

'You're beautiful too,' she said softly, and the blood roared through Zayed's veins. This woman enflamed him. He pulled her to him, wanting to be slow and deliberate but craving her too much, even now. Especially now.

They fell onto the bed in a tangle of limbs, hands and mouth reaching for whatever bit of skin they could access. He skimmed his hand along her inner thigh and she bucked, her response overwhelming.

Zayed reached for a condom from his bedside table. This time he would be careful. Within moments he'd buried himself inside her and, as Olivia met him thrust for thrust, he forgot about everything…everything but her.

CHAPTER ELEVEN

'HERE YOU ARE.'

Olivia took the slim rectangular box and tried not to gulp as she stared down at the lettering on its front. Zayed met her uncertain gaze evenly, his face completely bland, grey-green eyes shuttered. She'd spent all last night lost in his arms, seeking and finding pleasure after pleasure and joy after joy, but right now she had no idea what he was thinking or feeling, and she lacked the courage to ask him. A depressing thought, considering how wonderfully intimate last night had been—far more than the last two occasions they had come together.

Even now, with Zayed standing so fathomlessly in front of her, Olivia remembered how tenderly he'd held her, the Arabic endearments he'd murmured in her ear, the way he'd touched her, so reverently, as if she were a cherished treasure…and that was how she'd felt. She'd slept in his arms all night and woken in the morning with the biggest smile on her face and in her heart.

This moment was another proposition entirely.

'Should I...?' She glanced down at the rather lurid pink and blue writing on the side of the box. 'Should I take it now?'

'I don't see why not.' Zayed's voice was as bland as his face, yet in both she detected an intensity that alarmed her. Was he dreading the possibility of her being pregnant that much? If she was pregnant, would he feel trapped, tied to her in a way he might hate?

'Right.' Her numb fingers closed around the box. 'Well, then...'

He nodded towards the en-suite bathroom. 'I'll wait here.'

Wordlessly Olivia nodded, then she turned and made for the bathroom, closing the door behind her with a final-sounding click. She laid the box on the edge of the sink, willing her heart rate to slow and her nerves to steady. She was so nervous, and she had a terrible feeling it was because she was scared she wasn't pregnant. That she'd be sent away. Or was she worried that she was pregnant and would be made to stay? The trouble was, Olivia didn't know which she felt. Everything was a churning, mixed-up jumble inside her, and Zayed's inscrutable face and tone weren't helping.

Still, there was no point analysing her emotions until she knew the truth of the matter. Taking a deep breath, Olivia opened the box.

Three minutes later she turned over the test she'd taken to read the results, her nerves and hand both surprisingly steady. Three minutes had been an agony to wait, but now that the time had come she felt calmer because she knew she wanted to know, needed to know, for her own sake, her own sanity. She couldn't take any more limbo. Even so, the single line, stark and vivid, felt like a smack in the face, a fist to the gut.

One line. Not pregnant.

Olivia sank down onto the edge of the sunken tub, her heart plummeting like a stone. Disappointment. That was what she felt now—like a tidal wave crashing over her and pulling her under. Total, sick disappointment. Tears stung her eyes and, impatient with herself, she blinked them away. This was a good thing. It had to be.

If she'd been pregnant, Zayed would have felt honour-bound to keep her as his wife, and theirs would have been a marriage of expediency and growing resentment, hardly the kind of environment in which to raise a child, never mind find her own happiness.

She took a deep breath and let it out slowly. Yes, this was better. Even if her heart now felt like a leaden weight inside her, dragging her down.

'Olivia?' Zayed rapped on the door. 'Surely you must have taken the test by now?'

'Yes.' She couldn't let the disappointment show on her face, Olivia realised with a jolt of panic. That would be far too humiliating, to have Zayed realise she'd wanted his baby. She'd wanted to stay. 'Yes, I've taken it.'

'Well?' Zayed sounded impatient, and Olivia couldn't tell if there was any other emotion underneath that, hope or fear or something else.

'I'm coming out.' She glanced at the test one last time, the single, stark line, and then threw it into the bin. As she washed her hands she gave herself a silent and stern talking-to in the mirror.

This is for the best. It really is. You know that, Olivia, in your head, if not in your heart. You wouldn't want Zayed to feel trapped. You wouldn't want to feel trapped.

'Olivia,' Zayed prompted, a definite edge to his voice. She opened the door. His narrowed gaze scanned her from head to foot, assessing. 'Well?'

'I'm not pregnant,' Olivia said quietly. Thankfully her voice was steady, as were her hands, which she folded in front of her.

'You're not?' Zayed sounded surprised. 'But...'

'But what? This was the most likely outcome, really.' She made her mouth turn up in a smile. 'It's a relief for both of us, I'm sure.'

'Yes.' Zayed's lips pressed together in a firm line. 'Yes,' he said again.

Olivia took a deep breath, willing this moment onward. 'So,' she said, prompting him to make that painful cut she knew was necessary. Zayed simply stared at her, eyes still narrowed. 'You will resume negotiations with Sultan Hassan,' Olivia continued. 'And I will...' She paused, wondering just what she would do. Where she would go from here. The future felt like a void. 'I'll make my plans.'

Zayed's eyes narrowed further, to silvery-green slits. 'And what plans are you thinking of making?'

Olivia tilted her chin. 'That's not your concern any more, is it?'

'You're my wife. Of course it's my concern.'

'Don't, Zayed.' She didn't think she could take one of his autocratic dictates right now, never mind his playing the marriage card. 'You know I'm not your wife like that.' Never like that.

'You're my wife in every way possible at the

moment,' Zayed returned. 'Or have you forgotten last night?' Heat simmered in his eyes and Olivia felt as if the very air between them had tautened.

Olivia knew she'd live with the memory of last night for the rest of her life. 'Of course I haven't.'

'Until this issue is resolved to my satisfaction, you will make no plans,' Zayed ordered.

'Your satisfaction?' Was he actually going to keep her prisoner? She didn't think she could bear it. 'And what about mine?'

'And yours,' Zayed allowed. 'I will make sure you are provided for, no matter what. But we are not finished here, Olivia. Not yet.'

'How can we not be?' His words, flatly delivered as they were, offered her a shred of hope that she knew she should refuse. Far better for him to release her, free her, so she could start to recover and heal. Staying with him would prolong the agony of wanting something she now knew she could never have. 'You need to focus on Princess Halina,' Olivia pressed on. 'And Sultan Hassan. I'm no help there, Zayed.'

'You might be. Princess Halina might want to speak with you.'

'And do you want that?' she challenged. What on earth could she say to Halina that her friend wanted to hear? The conversation would be devastating for them both.

'In any case,' Zayed said, 'Sultan Hassan has taken Halina to Italy and is refusing my messages as well as any possible meeting. I cannot resume any marriage negotiations at the moment.'

She stared at him, surprised at how unperturbed he seemed by the situation, when he'd already told her more than once how essential this marriage alliance was. 'Then...what will you do?'

Zayed stared at her for a long moment, his gaze considering. Olivia held her breath, although she wasn't even sure why. It felt as if they were on the precipice of something important, but what?

'I rather thought,' he said slowly, 'I might stay married to you.'

The words echoed through her, reverberating for several endless moments. 'You rather thought?' she repeated in numb disbelief, even as she tried to tamp down the absurd happiness spiralling inside her. 'Do I have no say in the matter, then?'

'Of course you do.' Impatience flickered across Zayed's face and then he deliberately relaxed, offered her a smile. 'That's why I'm discussing it with you now.'

Olivia blew out a breath. 'I didn't realise this was a discussion.'

'Let's not quibble about semantics.' He crossed the room to sit on a divan by the window, one leg elegantly crossed over the other. 'Let's have a reasonable, measured conversation.'

About marriage. Because, of course, this was going to be a business arrangement, just like his marriage to Halina would have been.

'All right.' Olivia moved over to the sofa flanking his and sank onto it. 'Tell me what you're considering, then.'

Zayed glanced at Olivia; she sat with her ankles crossed and her hands folded in her lap, like a nun awaiting her orders. Zayed knew he needed to handle this with both care and sensitivity. What seemed obvious and easy to him would not necessarily be so to Olivia.

'It's come to my attention that having a western wife with a background in diplomacy is no bad thing.'

'A background in diplomacy?' Her eyebrows rose. 'I'd hardly give myself so much credit. My father was a diplomat, yes, a minor one, but I never was.'

'Still, you speak several languages; you've lived in many countries. Whether you realise it or not, Olivia, you are a woman of the world.'

She looked away, colour touching her cheeks. 'With very little experience of anything.'

'You were as at ease with the tribe's women a few weeks ago as you were with Serrat last night. Your lack of worldly experience does not discredit you.'

She shook her head, her gaze still averted. 'What of the marriage alliance that was so essential to you?'

'I took a risk when I attempted to kidnap Princess Halina. A knowing risk. It hasn't worked out, so I can look elsewhere.'

'Elsewhere?'

'To France and other European countries. If they support my claim, I don't need Hassan.'

'You don't need me, either.'

'Not in the same way, perhaps,' Zayed said after a moment. Jahmal had raised the same issue when Zayed had broached his proposition a few days ago. Surely, his aide had argued, there were other, more suitable women to be the Sultan's bride? In Jahmal's eyes Olivia was still nothing but a servant, even though Zayed knew he'd come both to like and admire her over the last few weeks.

Olivia turned back to face him, resolute now. 'In what way, Zayed?' she asked quietly. 'In what way do you need me?'

It felt like a loaded question. Was she acting

from the practical, pragmatic viewpoint he was determined to keep with regard to marriage, or was she asking about something more? About need…the way he'd needed her last night? Love, even? Zayed couldn't tell anything from her face; her eyes were a stormy blue, her mouth compressed.

'We are already married,' he said, knowing he was prevaricating but unsure how to deal with her in this mood. She seemed very quiet and self-contained, her head slightly bowed.

'Yes, but you were willing to set me aside before. Why not now?'

Zayed felt an uncomfortable twinge of guilt at those simply stated words. Yes, he'd been willing to put her aside. He'd had to be. But he felt differently now…and he realised he didn't particularly like Olivia asking him why.

'I've seen the advantages of our alliance,' he finally said. 'And since we are already married, and divorce or annulment is no small matter, it makes sense to stay married. Besides,' he added, watching her, 'we have a certain chemistry, do we not? That is no small thing.'

'I wouldn't know,' Olivia answered shortly.

'Nor perhaps would I,' Zayed agreed with a small smile. He longed to lighten her mood; he wanted her to be happy about this, damn it. 'Before you, Olivia, I had not been with a woman since my days at Cambridge.'

He'd surprised her with that. 'Ten years? I know you said it had been a long time...'

'As long as that.' He shrugged. 'My point is, we are good together. You are an asset to me.'

'As asset,' she repeated, and he had a feeling he'd chosen the wrong word.

'I would be honoured,' he said a bit tightly, 'to have you as my wife.'

A tiny smile curved her mouth, lightened her eyes. 'Is that a proposal?'

'After the fact, but yes.' He waited, feeling tenser than he wanted to be. Her answer mattered to him very much. He'd been hoping she was pregnant, and then there would have needed to be no discussion. The matter would have been resolved. As it was, he needed to convince her of the merits of their marriage. And if she said no? Would he let her go? The possibility caused him an unexpectedly strong wrench of feeling.

Olivia pursed her lips, her expression distant. 'What kind of marriage would we have?' she asked after a long, taut moment of waiting.

'The kind anyone has. A real marriage in every sense of the word.'

'Real?' She finally met his gaze, her own startlingly direct. 'A real marriage means a loving one.'

He recoiled a little, unable to keep himself from it. 'Is that what you want? Love?'

Her mouth twisted in a sad smile. 'I've dreamed of it, yes. I think most young girls do.'

'True.' He hesitated, wanting to appease her but knowing he could make no promises to love her. None at all.

'I know you don't love me, Zayed,' Olivia said. She almost sounded gentle. 'I'm not expecting you to proclaim your love or something like that.' She laughed softly. 'The expression on your face! You look horrified.'

Zayed tried to school his features into something more appropriate. 'I'm sorry.'

'It's all right.' She sighed and leaned back against the sofa. 'I just have to consider if it's something I'm willing to give up.'

'There are worse things than being a slave to such an emotion.'

She glanced at him curiously. 'Is that how you see it? As some form of slavery?'

Zayed shrugged. 'It traps you. Takes you hostage.'

'You've been in love, then?'

'No, not romantically. But I've lost people I've loved, and I don't want to feel that… vulnerable again.' His hands tightened into fists. He felt vulnerable enough just admitting that much.

Olivia nodded slowly. 'I suppose I can understand that.'

'Can you?' He felt a wave of relief, then a flicker of hope. 'Then…?'

'I need to think about it,' Olivia said. 'We're talking about a life decision, Zayed, not something to be decided in a moment.'

'Of course.'

'Although I understand your need to have this issue resolved as quickly as possible.'

He smiled, letting it linger. 'Your understanding is very considerate, Olivia.'

She smiled back, and there it was, the spark that always seemed to be snapping between them, kindling into flame. He wanted her all over again, and he let her see it in his eyes.

'We would be good together, Olivia. We *are* good together.'

'In that way,' she murmured, looking away. 'Yes.'

'It is not to be discounted.' He paused, wanting to convince her, to seal the deal, no matter what she said about needing to think. 'I believe I could make you happy.' He realised as he spoke the words that he meant them. He could make her happy and, moreover, he wanted to make her happy. Over the last few weeks he'd enjoyed seeing that shy smile bloom across her face. Last night he'd loved feeling her come alive in his arms. She'd lived a quiet, sheltered life, a life of restraint and shadows. He would be able to give her so much more once he was restored to his throne. And he would be restored. Soon. Very soon.

Olivia nodded, seeming lost in thought, her gaze averted from his. Zayed wished he knew what she was thinking. He wished he knew how to convince her.

'Why don't you come with me tomorrow?' he said impulsively. Olivia at least turned back to look at him.

'Come with you? Where?'

'I'm touring some nearby villages, to reassure the people.'

Olivia frowned. 'Should you really have me accompany you when it hasn't been decided?'

Probably not, but Zayed wanted her there. Wanted to show his people as well as Olivia herself that she could be his Queen. That she was his Queen.

'It would be an opportunity for you to see what your role would be, and for my people to see you.'

'And if we dissolve the marriage...?'

He shrugged. 'Then I will explain.' He leaned forward, urgent now. 'But give us a chance, Olivia. Give Kalidar a chance.'

Olivia let out a long, low breath and nodded

slowly. 'All right,' she said, and it sounded like a concession rather than something she might look forward to. 'I'll go with you.'

CHAPTER TWELVE

THE WIND WHIPPED Olivia's hair away from her face as the Jeep bumped over the desert dunes. They'd touched down in a helicopter an hour ago and had been travelling steadily since then under a bright blue sky and lemon-yellow sun. After the cool alpine temperatures at Rubyhan, the desert heat felt overwhelming, like entering a furnace. At least the breeze from the open-top Jeep helped.

Besides being hot, Olivia felt bone-achingly tired. She had barely slept at all last night, her mind going round in dizzying circles as she considered Zayed's 'proposal,' unromantic and businesslike as it had been. What had she been expecting? That he'd confess he'd fallen in love with her? She'd known all along Zayed wasn't interested in that. His duty was to his country and his people and, if marriage to her helped those two things, then he would pursue it.

But would she?

That was the question she was afraid to answer. Afraid to want.

Zayed glanced back at her, a reassuring smile curving his mouth, his eyes glinting in the harsh desert light. 'We will be there soon.' He touched her hand briefly, and even that sent sparks racing along her nerve endings. No, she supposed, just as Zayed had said, their physical chemistry was not to be underestimated. But was it enough?

The Jeep continued to bump along and Olivia leaned back against the seat, closing her eyes against the stunning view and the questions that thudded relentlessly through her. She had no answers, which was why she hadn't had any sleep last night.

After another twenty minutes or so the Jeep slowed down and Olivia opened her eyes to see they were on the edge of a small village of single storey, mud-brick dwellings. Most of the village had come out to greet them, wide smiles and curious eyes for their future King and the woman accompanying him. His future Queen. Could she really be that person? Did she want to be?

Zayed got out of the Jeep first, waving at the crowd who had gathered before turning to open the door for Olivia.

'Who will they think I am?' she whispered

as she took his hand and clambered out of the vehicle.

'My Queen,' Zayed said simply. 'Because that is who you are.'

'Zayed…' This was not the place to discuss the future, yet already Olivia felt trapped; a noose, tempting as it was, was tightening about her neck. Had Zayed invited her along today so it would be harder to back out? The more people who saw her as his Queen, the more she'd see herself that way? And the more people she'd disappoint if she walked away from all of this.

Such thoughts were swept away as Zayed led her to the crowd. She waved and saw the women sigh or look speculative; clearly everyone was wondering. But she couldn't let herself worry about that as the day went on and they moved from one festivity to another, inspecting a newly built school, listening to children sing, having glasses of tea with the head of the tribe.

By late afternoon Olivia was feeling tired and a bit overwhelmed, but also surprisingly happy. She had a role here, and one she was surprisingly good at. She liked chatting to people—her Arabic had improved over the last few weeks—and entering into their lives. After a lifetime spent in the shadows, she was finally, wonderfully, stepping into the light, in all sorts of ways, thanks to Zayed. Who would ever have thought a kidnapping would lead to self-awareness and fulfilment? And yet she knew now, whatever the future held, she would be a better, braver person for it…thanks to Zayed.

By nightfall she was ready to crawl into bed and sleep for hours. The women of the village had brought her to the finest house, and in it to a bedroom that was surprisingly sumptuous, considering how little the people of the village had. Olivia thanked them and then began to undress. She'd just taken off her headscarf and slipped out of the traditional kaftan she'd worn when the door to the bedroom opened.

Olivia whirled around, clutching the kaftan to her. 'Zayed…' His name came out in a surprised rush. 'What are you doing here?'

'Sleeping, as are you.'

'But…' She shook her head slowly. 'Then the people of the village know we are married?'

'It would seem so.' He seemed remarkably unperturbed.

'Did you tell them?'

'I did not tell them otherwise.'

Olivia sank onto the bed, the kaftan still clutched to her chest. 'Are you making it harder for me to say no?'

Zayed shrugged out of the linen *thobe* he wore, revealing his bronzed, muscled chest in all its perfection. 'Maybe,' he admitted, eyes glinting. 'As I've said before, Olivia, we're good together.'

'In bed.' She spoke flatly.

'In all ways. Today, for example. You were in your element out there.' His glinting gaze turned penetrating as he looked at her. 'You enjoyed it, didn't you? Talking to people, listening and learning? You've spent all of your adult life as a servant, silent and obedient, but you don't need to be like that any more.'

It was so close to what she'd been thinking earlier, so…why was she resisting? Why was she fighting what Zayed was offering, when it was so much more than she'd ever had before, ever hoped to have?

Olivia stared at him helplessly, knowing that she'd been resisting all along because she was afraid. Afraid of loving him as desperately as she knew she did while he felt only desire and perhaps affection for her.

Yet… *Would that be so bad?* Couldn't she live with it? She'd lived with less—far less— and she'd found a certain kind of happiness. She could have more of it with Zayed. He enjoyed her company, at least, and they *were* good in bed together. And when children came along and she was able to be a mother…

'Why fight it?' Zayed asked softly. 'Why fight us?'

'It's a big decision, Zayed,' Olivia answered, her voice shaky. 'And just because you've reached a certain conclusion doesn't mean I have.'

'But you are beginning to,' Zayed said, and there was certainty in his voice. 'You are.'

She opened her mouth but no words came out. She couldn't deny it. She wasn't even sure she wanted to. What was love, anyway? An ephemeral emotion, a will-o'-the-wisp, nothing you could hold onto, and perhaps nothing you could count on either. Zayed was offering her more than anyone else ever had. Why not take it? Why not grasp happiness while she could?

'Olivia,' he said, his voice full of warmth and promise. He reached for her and she came willingly, closing her eyes as their bodies brushed and collided. She leaned her head against his shoulder and they stood there, embracing, for several sweet moments.

I love you. The words came unbidden into her mind, hovered on her tongue. How had she fallen in love so quickly, so easily? Olivia closed her eyes, willing those treacherous words away. Zayed would not want to hear them. Not now, and most likely not ever.

With his arms around her, Zayed guided her towards the bed. Laughing, Olivia stumbled slightly, her leg brushing against something she assumed was the bed, but then she felt a sharp, stinging pain in her ankle. She gasped, and Zayed looked at her in surprise, but before Olivia could so much as open her mouth she felt a strange, numbing cold sweep over her body, and then she knew nothing at all.

'Olivia…?' Zayed stared at her in confusion—at her face, pale and shocked. 'What is it—'

Out of the corner of his eye he saw a movement and he jerked around to see the sinuous, black shape of a desert cobra slither across the darkened floor.

Zayed swore aloud and then he shouted for help. Already Olivia's body was going stiff, her eyes sightless. Quickly Zayed hoisted her onto the bed, looking for where she'd been bitten. He found the angry-looking fang marks on her ankle, and he tore off a strip from his *thobe* to tie around her leg and isolate the venom, praying that he wasn't too late.

Seconds later Jahmal burst into the room, followed by several of his armed guards.

'What is it? What has happened?'

'Snakebite,' Zayed said tersely. 'Do we have an antivenom injection in the Jeep?'

'I'll get it.' Jahmal left quickly, while Zayed stared down at Olivia, her body jerking in response to the venom flowing through her system, her gaze blank and unresponsive. Cobra bites were some of the most dangerous in the world, with a high mortality rate, especially in such remote areas as this.

Damn it, why hadn't he checked for snakes? After ten years of living in the desert, he was used to doing it, but he'd been so consumed by Olivia, by the promise he'd seen in her eyes, that he'd forgotten. And now he stood here, helpless, holding her hand, her life at stake, *his* life at stake…because she was his life. The realisation cut through him cleanly, leaving him dazed and reeling.

He loved her, Zayed acknowledged with a terrible, sinking sensation, and once again he was going to have to stand by and watch as the person he loved most in the world suffered and died. It was more than he could bear. Not again. Not ever.

'Hold on, Olivia,' he whispered, trying to imbue her with his own strength. *'Hold on.'*

The next few hours passed in a blur of grief and fear. Jahmal administered the antivenom medication, and Zayed watched, utterly helpless as Olivia writhed and retched, so clearly suffering and in pain that Zayed felt as if his own body, his own heart, were being rent apart. He wished he could take her pain, longed to ease her suffering, but just as before, just as always, there was nothing he could do. And he didn't know if he could live through that again.

'Will she survive?' he asked the doctor he'd flown in from Arjah, thirty-six hours after Olivia had first been bitten. Zayed had barely left her bedside in all that time.

The doctor gave him a sorrowful smile and shrugged. 'It is impossible to say. A snakebite... As a man of the desert, Prince Zayed, you know how dangerous and even deadly these can be.'

'Yes, I know.' Zayed's hands curled into fists. 'But a person can survive if the venom hasn't spread.'

'Yes, and we will not know whether that has happened.' The doctor dared to lay a hand on his arm. 'If it is fatal, it will be soon. We will have an answer in the next day or two.'

An answer Zayed couldn't bear to think about.

Forty-eight hours after the serpent had first slithered away, Olivia stirred and then opened her eyes. She licked dry lips, her unfocused gaze moving around the room. Zayed leaned forward.

'Habibi...' The endearment slipped from his lips unthinkingly. He reached for her hand. 'You're awake.'

Slowly, as if the movement made everything in her ache, Olivia turned her head to look at him, her expression still dazed. She opened her mouth to speak but only a sigh came out.

'Don't speak,' Zayed urged her. 'Don't strain yourself, not now.' Relief broke over him like a wave on the shore, followed by a deep, unsettling unease. If she was awake, if she was cognisant, she had survived. She *would* survive. And, as grateful as Zayed was for Olivia's life, he didn't know if he had it in him to withstand something like this again. How many risks would he have to take? He'd live his whole life in jeopardy, in fear, for the one he loved. For the heart that could break.

Back in his own room, Jahmal was waiting with a grim look on his face, having just returned from Rubyhan. Zayed glanced at him, both irritated and alarmed by his aide's gloomy face.

'What?' he demanded. He hadn't slept in over two days and his mind was a haze of physical and emotional fatigue. 'Why are you looking like the walls have come crashing down?'

'Perhaps because they have, Prince Zayed.'

Zayed stilled in the action of taking off the linen *thobe* he'd worn for far too long; he hadn't bothered to change his clothes since Olivia had been hurt. 'What do you mean?'

'There was a message from Serrat back at Rubyhan. He says he is sorry, but his government is not willing to support your claim at this point.'

Zayed sat heavily on the bed and raked his hands through his hair. After the success of the dinner with Serrat, he had hoped for better. Hell, he'd expected it.

'Did he say why?'

'He gave no reason, My Prince.'

Zayed nodded slowly. 'There will be others.' But it was a blow—a big blow—that woke him from the stupor of grief and fear he'd been in for the last two days.

'You should return to Rubyhan,' Jahmal urged. 'Speak to Serrat and reach out to Sultan Hassan again, before Malouf hears of these developments and grows even bolder.'

'But Olivia…' The words died on Zayed's lips as he caught sight of his aide's face, and the flicker of something almost like contempt that went across it. He was a prince—would be the King when he could return to Arjah and be crowned. He was a leader of men, of a people, a country, and he had a duty to them, to the memory of his family…and that came before any duty he had to his mistaken bride. Besides, Olivia was getting better, and the greatest danger was past.

He gave Jahmal a terse nod. 'Be ready to leave within the hour.' Zayed did not miss the relief that broke across Jahmal's face before he turned away.

After washing and dressing in a fresh *thobe*, Zayed went in search of the doctor.

'She seems better,' he said, part-statement, part-question, and the man nodded.

'Yes, the worst is past. But it will be some days before I can discover whether there has been lasting damage.'

Zayed's stomach clenched. 'What kind of lasting damage?'

'To organs, muscles, even the brain. I am hopeful, my Prince, that the venom did not spread so far, but I can make no promises at this juncture.'

'Of course.' Dread swirled in his stomach at the thought of Olivia facing such damage…and it would be his fault. His fault for bringing her here, for kidnapping her in the first place. 'Give her the best care,' he instructed. 'And, when she is well enough, arrange for her transport back to Rubyhan.'

The man nodded. 'It will be done.'

Jahmal was waiting in the Jeep when Zayed slipped into Olivia's room for a private fare-well. She was asleep, her face pale, her dark hair spread over the pillow, her lashes sweeping her cheeks. Her breathing was steady and yet so very light; she was barely a bump under the covers, her body fragile and slight.

Zayed sat next to her and took her limp hand

in his. A dozen different memories ran through his mind in a bittersweet reel: that first explosive night; the way she'd cared for the women and children after Malouf's attack. Seeing her in the palace garden, Lahela's baby on her lap, looking so happy. The way she'd given herself to him, so freely and utterly. The stormy blue of her eyes, the sudden surprise of her smile. His insides twisted in an agony of indecision. Love *hurt*.

He didn't want to leave her, but he knew he had to. And perhaps it was better this way; he'd never meant to love her, never meant to open himself to that kind of pain again. If he left now, he could gain the emotional distance he needed and so could she. Yes, it was better this way. Better for both of them.

Zayed squeezed Olivia's hand gently and then brushed a kiss against her forehead. As he eased back, her eyelids flickered, but before she could open them properly she'd lapsed back into sleep.

With a wrenching pain feeling as if it were tearing him in two, Zayed backed out of the room and then headed for the Jeep, Rubyhan and the rest of his life.

CHAPTER THIRTEEN

OLIVIA WOKE SLOWLY, as if she were swimming up to the surface of the sea, the light shimmering and sparkling in the distance. Someone was speaking to her, saying her name, and she felt fingers on her wrist.

Her eyelids felt heavy, as if someone had placed weights on them. As much as she tried, she could not open them.

Olivia... Olivia...

Waves of fatigue rolled over her, making it even harder to hear that voice. Every muscle in her body ached, so she felt as if she'd been ruthlessly pummelled and punched. All she wanted to do was sleep, and so she did.

When she woke again the room was lost in twilit shadows, and although she still felt that overwhelming fatigue she was able to open her eyes. A man was sitting by her bed. In the shadowy darkness she thought it was Zayed and her heart leapt.

'Zayed…'

'No, Miss Taylor. I am Ammar Abdul, the Prince's doctor.'

'Oh.' As her eyes adjusted to the dim room, she could see the man, tall and thin, looking nothing like Zayed. 'Where…where is Zayed?'

'Prince Zayed has returned to Rubyhan.' There was a faintly repressive note to the doctor's voice that made Olivia realise her question had been presumptuous.

'I…see.' Her mouth felt terribly dry. 'Could I have a drink of water?'

'Of course.' With alacrity the doctor rose and poured her a glass of water from the pitcher on the bedside table, held it to her lips. Olivia took several grateful sips before subsiding back on the pillow, exhausted by even that small amount of activity.

'What…what has happened to me?' she asked. The last thing she remembered was Zayed taking her in his arms, telling her not to fight him. Not to fight them.

Tears pricked her eyes; her emotions felt so very raw, right up at the surface of everything. Why had he left her?

'You were bitten by a snake, Miss Taylor. A desert cobra. You are fortunate to be alive.'

A snake. Briefly, distantly, Olivia remembered the stinging pain in her ankle. 'How... how long have I been like this?'

'It has been four days since you were bitten. For some time we did not know whether you would live or die. As I said, you are very fortunate.'

'Thank you,' she murmured. 'How much longer will I be here?'

'Prince Zayed wishes you to return to Rubyhan as soon as it is safe to do so, perhaps in another day.'

Olivia nodded, and after a few moments the doctor left her to rest. She stared into the darkness, her heart a leaden weight inside her. Four days, and her life at stake. And Zayed had left. No matter why or when, she couldn't ignore that fact. She couldn't move past it.

He never promised to love you, she reminded herself. *He has a kingdom to run.*

But the fact that he wasn't here, that he'd chosen not to be here, felt like a hammer to her fragile hopes. It was a wake-up call to the reality of what she'd been about to agree to, and a much-needed one at that.

Olivia spent the day resting and trying to recover, and by the next morning Ammar Abdul deemed her well enough to be transported back to Rubyhan.

'It does not appear that you will have any

lasting effects from the snakebite,' he told her after he'd checked her over. 'But you will require another complete check in a few weeks to make sure. In the meantime, rest, sleep, eat and drink.' He gave her a smile with sympathy. 'You will feel a little better each day.'

'That's good to hear.' She felt about a hundred years old at the moment, moving slowly, everything aching. The ride in the Jeep was torture, with all the bumps and jostling, and the short helicopter ride to Rubyhan was no better. By the time Olivia arrived at the Palace of Clouds, she was exhausted and aching more than ever, longing only for her bed...and Zayed.

He was not waiting at the helipad when she touched down and she didn't see him as Anna escorted her into the palace. Although she knew she probably shouldn't, Olivia couldn't keep from asking about him.

'How is Prince Zayed?'

Anna gave her a brief, inscrutable look. 'He is quite busy at the moment, dealing with various issues of diplomacy, but I will let him know that you have arrived.'

'Thank you,' Olivia murmured, fighting that bone-deep disappointment she'd felt since she'd woken up and realised that Zayed was gone. That he didn't care. Or was she being unreasonable, expecting him to sit by her bedside like some lovesick nurse? He had a country to run, duties to perform. She was being over-emotional and ridiculous, but she couldn't help herself.

It was another full day before she actually saw Zayed. She'd spent most of her time in her room, resting or sleeping, trying to manage a few meals although she had no appetite. Then, the evening of her second day back at Rubyhan, Anna fetched her.

'Prince Zayed would like to see you now,' she said, and Olivia suppressed the sarcastic reply she wanted to make: *what, now?* He beckoned and she came, apparently.

Anna led her not to one of Zayed's private, more casual rooms, but to a formal audience chamber on the ground floor, with marble pillars and walls adorned with gold leaf. Zayed stood at the far end of the room, dressed in a traditional *thobe*, embroidered with red and blue thread, and loose trousers. He could not have shown her more thoroughly that he wanted to create a distance between them.

What had changed since he'd drawn her in his arms and told her how good they were together? What had happened?

Anna quietly closed the door behind her so Olivia was alone with Zayed—Prince Zayed, because that was how this felt. He was the

Prince and she was the commoner. She swallowed hard and walked slowly to one of the gilt-covered chairs at the side of the room.

'You'll have to excuse me,' she said stiffly. 'I still cannot stand for long periods.'

'Of course you must sit.' Zayed took a step forward and then stopped as Olivia sank into a chair. His gaze, as unreadable as ever, swept over her. 'You are looking far better than when I last saw you.'

'And when was that?' Olivia returned, a touch sharply. Zayed frowned and she looked away, biting her lip. There was no point in revealing her hurt feelings. It was clear they didn't matter.

'Five days ago.' Zayed's voice was cool. 'I had to return to Rubyhan on official matters.'

'Of course.' Neither of them spoke, the silence between them a heavy burden that Olivia didn't have the strength to bear. Not now, and maybe never. 'What's happened, Zayed?' she asked quietly. 'What has changed?'

'Changed?'

'Between us.' She met his gaze directly, unafraid now. How much more could he hurt her? 'I don't remember much after the snake bit me, but I remember before. I remember you telling me to fight for us and drawing me into your arms.' She swallowed. 'Then, the next thing I know, I've been desperately ill for four days and you're back in Rubyhan. I arrived yesterday morning and this is the first I've even seen you.'

Zayed's jaw was tight. 'I've been busy.'

'And when I do see you, it's as if I'm some supplicant coming to beg a favour from the king.' She gestured to the ornate reception room. 'What is this? What are you trying to tell me?'

Zayed was silent for a long moment and Olivia waited, holding her breath, because there was something. She just didn't know what it was.

'I've heard from Serrat,' Zayed said at last.

'Serrat? The French diplomat?'

'Yes.'

'And?' She searched his face, finding nothing, feeling cold. 'What did he say?'

'France is not willing to support my claim.'

'Oh. I'm sorry.' She absorbed the statement for a few seconds and then realised what it meant for her. 'You are questioning whether my credentials matter any longer,' she said slowly. Zayed didn't answer. 'Whether a western wife who can speak French and has a background in foreign service matters at all.' It was suddenly so obvious and it hurt so much. Far more than she wanted it to. She nodded slowly, accepting, because what other choice did she have? She loved him, but he didn't love her. She'd known that all along. 'So, back to plan A?' she asked with an attempt at levity that fell entirely flat.

'There's more.' Zayed bit the words off, his jaw clenched tight. 'Sultan Hassan has been in contact.'

'Ah.' She leaned back and folded her arms. 'His temper has cooled off, I suppose?'

'Something like that. He wishes to discuss my engagement to Princess Halina.'

'Right.' So it was all happening for him. She was no longer needed. And suddenly Olivia realised she was glad. No, not glad, never that, but relieved, because at least this had happened now and not in months or years, when the prospect of being set aside would have been utterly devastating. Her heart was broken, but it would mend. She would make sure of it. 'Then all that remains is for me to book my plane ticket to Paris.' Her lips trembled and she pressed them together, determined not to cry. Not to reveal one shred of heartbreak to Zayed. Not when he so clearly didn't care at all.

'I will arrange it for you,' he said after a brief, tense pause. 'But first I must ask you to do one last thing.'

'Which is?' Olivia asked, although she could guess already.

'To accompany me to Abkar. Princess Halina wishes to see you, as does Sultan Hassan.'

Olivia squeezed her eyes shut, steeling herself against the pain, and then snapped them open again. She could do this. She could survive. 'Fine,' she said, her voice as terse as Zayed's. 'When do we leave?'

This felt all wrong. Zayed gazed at Olivia's pale, heart-shaped face and wanted nothing more than to sweep her into his arms and never let her go. Seeing her walk into the room, standing, recovered, *alive*, had been almost too much to bear. The last five days had been utter hell, the news from France and Abkar overridden by his fear and concern for Olivia. He'd had hourly reports on her condition from Ammar Abdul, and he hadn't cared how it had made him look.

But he'd still arrived at this moment and brought Olivia with him. Whatever had been between them was over. He had to put his country first. His duty first. The memory of his father and brother spiralling down to their death, his mother in his arms, they came first. They had to. The news of Hassan's renewed interest on top of Serrat backing away had felt like an omen, a wake-up call. He had to stop pursuing his own pleasure, his own happiness, and do what was best for Kalidar.

'We'll leave tomorrow,' he said. 'The visit should be brief.' He paused, swallowing past the jagged lump that had formed in his throat. 'You can be in Paris in a few days.'

Zayed didn't see Olivia until they were boarding the helicopter the next morning. He'd barely slept all night, wanting only to go to her. One last night in her arms, forbidden and sweet. He didn't, because he knew it wouldn't be fair to her, or Princess Halina, for that matter. The break needed to be clean, quick and final.

They didn't speak on the helicopter ride from Rubyhan, or in the armoured car they took through the desert to Abkar. Olivia's face was turned to the window as the dunes slid by, and after several hours they arrived on the outskirts of Abkar's capital, the single-storey dwellings giving way to apartment buildings and high rises.

When the palace walls came into view, built of golden stone and interspersed with minarets, she let out a little sigh. 'It feels like a lifetime,' she said quietly.

It was a lifetime. A part of him had come to life in the last few weeks, and then died. The grief he felt was for that part of him as much as it was for losing Olivia. He didn't want to go back to the man he'd been, closed off from emotions, an island of independence and strength. He wanted to need her but he knew he couldn't.

Staff met them as soon as the car pulled up to the palace's front entrance. Zayed had barely a glance for Olivia before she was being ushered away, and he was taken to wait on Sultan Hassan in the palace's throne room.

The Sultan came quickly into the room, unsmiling, and Zayed gave him a brief nod, one head of state to another. The two men stared at each other for a long moment and then Hassan finally spoke.

'I do not applaud your methods, Prince Zayed, but at least you got my attention.'

'For that I am glad, Your Majesty.'

'It is unfortunate that you made such a grievous error.'

Zayed inclined his head. 'Indeed.' Part of him wanted to argue about the nature of that error, for Olivia was so much more to him than that, yet he did not. He couldn't.

'Under normal circumstances, I would not even receive you,' Hassan continued. 'While I understand your reasoning, as well as your intense desire to be restored to your kingdom, Princess Halina is my daughter, and a royal in her own right, and you attempted to treat her with immense disrespect.'

'I meant none, I assure you, Your Majesty.'

'Even so.' Hassan blew out an irritated breath. 'But the fact remains that the Princess's circumstances have changed.'

'Oh?' Zayed stood alert, a new wariness charging through him. What did Hassan mean?

He made it plain soon enough. 'Her mother took her to Italy a few weeks ago, to keep her out of the drama unfolding here,' Hassan said flatly. 'And it appears in that time that she got into trouble.'

'Trouble?'

'She is no longer a virgin,' Hassan stated, his face set like stone. 'In fact, she is pregnant with another man's child.' Shock ripped through Zayed, leaving him speechless for a few seconds. Hassan smiled grimly. 'It is not what you expected, I imagine.'

'I am taken by surprise,' Zayed admitted carefully.

'She has been dishonoured and ruined. The only way for her situation to be redeemed is for you to marry her as was originally planned. The child can be passed off as yours.'

Revulsion at such a cold-blooded suggestion made Zayed nearly recoil. 'And what of the biological father? Has he no interest in his child?'

'He has no say. He doesn't know, and I have no intention of him knowing.'

'Who is he?'

'That is not your concern.'

'On the contrary, it is most certainly my concern. You are asking me to raise his child as my own and potentially, if it is a son, to be my heir.'

'That is the price you must pay for your own misdeed,' Hassan returned coldly. 'Did you think I would forgive so easily? If you want my support, if you want to reclaim your kingdom, then you will do this one thing.'

Zayed took a quick, even breath, willing his temper to stay in check. Hassan had always been autocratic, assuming more authority and power than he'd ever truly possessed. Abkar was a small country, smaller even than Kalidar, although it was rich in resources and had a stable economy. But he would not take orders from the man. 'And what does the Princess think?'

'It is of no concern.'

'Even so, I would like to know.'

Hassan shrugged. 'You may ask her yourself. I will grant you a private audience with her later today.' His eyes flashed. 'You will take no liberties, I trust, or this offer will be rescinded.'

'Of course I will take no liberties.' Zayed knew he could hardly claim the moral high ground, but he'd forgotten, since his last interview with Hassan years ago, how much he disliked the man. He could be charming when he chose, but underneath that veneer of paternal kindness ran an arrogant, self-serving strain.

Hassan gave him a cold smile. 'Then we are finished here.'

A muscle ticked in Zayed's jaw. He realised he was furious—and not because of the other man's lack of respect for his title and position, the autocratic way he spoke, or the way he talked about his daughter, as if she were nothing more than a stain on his reputation. No, he was angry at this man, furious with him, because of his complete lack of concern for Olivia. She'd considered Hassan like a father. She'd viewed the palace as her home.

'You have not asked about Miss Taylor,' Zayed said, his voice low and level.

Hassan arched an eyebrow. 'And you, it seems, think I should have?'

'She has been a member of the royal household for four years.'

'She has been a servant, yes. I assume, Prince Zayed, that you have treated her comfortably?'

'Of course I have.' Zayed glared at the man, fighting an urge to throttle him.

'In any case, Miss Taylor is no longer a member of this household. Her position has been terminated. Understandably.'

'Will you give her a reference?'

Hassan's eyes glittered. 'I think not.'

It was just as Olivia had predicted, yet Zayed hated that this man, that anyone, thought so little of her.

Including yourself?

Pushing that most uncomfortable thought away, Zayed nodded once to Hassan then turned on his heel and left the room.

CHAPTER FOURTEEN

'*OLIVIA!*'

With a startled, '*Oof!*' Olivia put her arms around Halina as her friend rushed at her, hugging her tightly the minute she entered the small sitting room where Halina had been waiting for her arrival.

'Hello, Halina.'

'Are you all right? Have you been hurt? Has—has he hurt you?' Halina leaned back, sniffing, her eyes wide and frightened.

'I'm fine.'

'But you look so pale and tired.'

'I've been ill,' Olivia said briefly. 'But I've been treated with respect at all times.' With a tired smile she extricated herself from Halina's arms. She felt so very fragile, as if she could break, and it had nothing to do with her recovery from the cobra's bite. 'How are you? You've been in Italy, I heard?'

'Yes.' Halina bit her lip. 'Olivia, I'm afraid I've made a complete mess of things.'

'How so?' Olivia couldn't imagine how Halina could make things more of a mess than they already were. 'I think Zayed was the one who messed things up,' she added with an attempt at a wry smile, but it wobbled all over the place. She'd loved him, she still did, and he'd felt nothing for her. No matter how many times she ruthlessly hammered that truth home, it still hurt, the wound as fresh and deep as ever.

'Yes, but...' Tears filled Halina's eyes before she blinked them away. 'I made it all so much worse.'

Curious and a bit alarmed, Olivia shook her head. 'I don't understand, Halina.'

'When I went to Italy...' Halina broke off, turning away towards the window that overlooked the palace's landscaped gardens. 'I was so stupid,' she muttered, rubbing her temple with her fingers. 'So stupid and so naïve.'

'Halina...' Olivia took a step towards her old schoolfriend. 'You're scaring me a bit.'

'I've scared myself.' She let out a humourless laugh. 'I can't believe...'

'What happened?' Olivia asked gently. 'You can tell me.'

Halina took a deep, shuddering breath and then, turning around, she squared her shoulders. 'Mama took me to Italy, to a hotel in Rome, to get away from Abkar. Father was worried someone might attempt to kidnap me again. He didn't realise it was Prince Zayed, at least not at first, and then of course when he did he was furious.' She reached for Olivia, squeezing her arm. 'Was it awful, Livvy?' she asked, using the nickname from their school days. 'I'm so sorry.'

'It's not your fault,' Olivia said, her voice sounding funny. 'And it wasn't awful.' Halina must have seen something in her face—she could be remarkably perceptive at times—for her eyes narrowed, light dawning in their soft brown depths.

'What do you mean?'

'You were going to tell me what happened to you,' Olivia reminded her quickly. 'In Italy.'

Halina's shoulders slumped briefly. 'Yes, although I'm too ashamed to say. I thought I was so much more worldly than I really was— than I am. I was a *joke*.'

'What do you mean, Halina? Tell me what happened.'

'I snuck out of my hotel room,' Halina confessed, her face full of misery. 'And I slipped into a party being held downstairs. I just wanted a tiny bit of excitement, that was all. It didn't seem like so much.'

Which was what Olivia had wanted when she'd chosen to surrender to Zayed that first magical night. 'And what happened at the party?'

Olivia asked in a hollow voice. She had a feeling she could guess, yet she could scarcely believe it.

'I met someone. A man. A handsome devil of a man.' Halina sniffed. 'Olivia, I spent the night with him,' she confessed in a near wail. 'I slept with him. Lost my virginity to…to a stranger! I don't know what came over me. I wasn't even thinking. I thought I could handle it all, handle him, and of course I couldn't.'

'You don't mean he—'

'Forced me?' Halina gave a bitter laugh. 'Not a bit of it. I was completely willing—eager, even—and spinning stories in my head of I don't know what.' She shook her head. 'And then one of the royal guards found us.'

'Oh, Halina,' Olivia murmured, full of sympathy for her friend, yet finding it hard to believe they'd both succumbed to the same kind of overwhelming temptation. 'I'm so sorry.'

'That's not the worst of it,' Halina returned grimly. She sank onto a sofa, her head in her hands. 'Father made me take a pregnancy test a few days ago and guess what?' She let out a sound that was half laugh, half sob. 'I'm pregnant.'

'Oh, my goodness.' Shocked, Olivia sat onto the sofa next to Halina and put her arm around her. Halina leaned her head against Olivia's shoulder, drawing in a few ragged breaths.

'He was so, so angry, and I can't even blame him,' Halina said in a tear-filled voice. 'I've made a mess of everything.'

'And what of this man in Italy? Surely he has something to do with it?'

'He doesn't even know I'm pregnant,' Halina admitted. 'And Father won't tell him.'

'Why not?'

She lifted her head, wiping the tears from her long-lashed eyes. 'Because he wants Prince Zayed to accept the child as his own,' she said. 'What is he like, Olivia? Is he a savage? To think he wanted to kidnap me.' She shuddered. 'And now I'm meant to marry him.'

Abruptly Olivia rose from the sofa and crossed to the window, not wanting Halina to see the expression on her face. Not knowing how she felt about any of it: Zayed to pass off another child as his own, and marry Halina when he didn't love her and she obviously didn't even know him. It was so awful, so unjust, but it was what Zayed had chosen. It was what he wanted. Not love, and not her.

'What is it?' Halina asked after a moment. 'You've gone all strange and silent. What are you not telling me, Olivia?'

'Nothing.' Even to her own ears Olivia's voice sounded distant and strained.

'No, there's something; I can tell. I know

you, Olivia. I've known you since we were both eleven years old. What are you not telling me about Prince Zayed? Is it something terrible?'

'No, nothing like that.' Olivia dragged a breath into her lungs. 'He's…he's a good man, Halina.'

There was a tense moment of silence, and Olivia willed Halina to believe her, to be satisfied and for this conversation finally to be over, because she didn't think she could manage much more.

'You love him,' Halina said slowly. 'It's so obvious now that I can see it. You've fallen in love with him.'

'I haven't,' Olivia said, but her denial was so feeble she knew it wouldn't fool anyone, not even a child.

'You're in love with him, and he's meant to marry me!' Halina exclaimed, her voice filled with dismay. 'This is *awful*.'

'Zayed wants your marriage to go forward,' Olivia insisted. 'What I feel doesn't matter. Trust me, Halina, I know that.'

'Matter to whom?' Halina demanded. 'It matters to you, and it matters to me. And, if you love him, it should matter to Zayed.'

'It doesn't,' Olivia said wretchedly. 'He's made that clear.'

'I haven't defied my father over this because

I knew I brought shame to him. But it's different now.'

'It isn't.' Alarm filled Olivia and she whirled around. 'Halina, please don't break the engagement. *Please.* Zayed needs the alliance with your country. Your father will have told him what happened in Italy and he will have accepted it. I know. Please don't do anything rash.'

'You love him,' Halina said slowly, 'and you still want him to marry me?'

'He doesn't love me,' Olivia answered flatly, 'and I don't want to be with a man who doesn't love me. So think of it this way, if you must—I'm choosing not to be with him.'

'Except it doesn't seem as if you have much choice in the matter.'

'Let things be, Halina, please.' Olivia's whole body sagged; she felt as if she could barely stand. 'I can't talk about this any more. I was ill recently, and I need to rest. But promise me you won't say anything to Zayed.'

'Anything at all?'

'About me. About what I feel.'

Halina sighed. 'I promise, if you really don't want me to. But does he know you love him, Olivia? Because—'

'Trust me, Halina, it doesn't matter.'

Halina nodded slowly. 'Then get some rest. I'll see you later.' She kissed Olivia's cheek and squeezed her hand. 'What a pair we are,' she whispered with a hint of her old dramatic impishness. 'Having such adventures.'

'Yes.' Olivia smiled wearily and walked from the room, skidding to a halt halfway down the corridor when she saw Zayed striding towards her.

'You've been with the Princess?' he asked, his agate gaze sweeping over her and revealing nothing.

'Yes.'

'She told you?'

'About her pregnancy? Yes. I'm sorry, Zayed.'

'I have no one to blame but myself. And I can hardly accuse the Princess of being impetuous when I was just as rash.' He sighed and rubbed his temple.

'Are you getting a migraine?' Olivia asked quietly.

'It will pass.' He dropped his hand and subjected her to a direct look. 'How are you? How are you holding up?'

Her heart was in pieces, and she ached everywhere it was possible to ache, but she wasn't going to tell any of that to Zayed. 'I'm fine.'

Zayed looked at her closely, as if he could chip away at the thin veneer of calm and control she'd managed to erect. 'Olivia…'

'I need some rest.' Olivia knew she couldn't

withstand his apology, not now, not ever. It would be better if she never saw Zayed al bin Nur again in her life.

She tried to move past him but he caught her arm, turning her to face him. Their faces were close, their hips brushed and, despite the ache in her heart, desire rushed through her veins. She felt herself melt, knew she was utterly helpless from the moment he touched her.

'I wish…' Zayed breathed, one palm coming up to cup her cheek. 'I wish things had been different.'

'But they aren't.' She forced the words out even though it felt as if they were tearing her in two.

'I know.' Zayed's gaze became hooded as it dipped to her mouth. Olivia tensed, straining for his kiss even though she knew she should resist. He brushed his lips across hers, once, twice, before settling on them for a moment, pressing hard, as if he were sealing her memory inside him. Olivia clutched at his shoulders, accepting the brand, needing it to sustain her, and then finally she wrenched away with a gasp.

'Your fiancée is waiting,' she choked out, then hurried down the hall.

Zayed waited a moment, until his breathing and libido were both under control, before he opened the doors and stepped into the sitting room where he knew Princess Halina was waiting.

She whirled around at his entrance, her eyes widening as she realised who it was. 'Prince Zayed.'

'Princess Halina.' He gazed at her for a long moment, trying to view her objectively. Yes, she was pretty—tumbled, ebony hair, wide brown eyes, a delectably curvy figure. But she wasn't Olivia, and that was all that mattered.

'You've met with my father,' Halina said, and her voice wavered.

'Yes. He told me what happened in Italy.'

She lowered her gaze, lashes sweeping her cheeks. 'And you are willing to accept the change in circumstances?'

'It seems I have no choice.'

Halina looked up, all modesty gone as her eyes flashed. 'Of all the people in this situation, Prince Zayed, you have the most choice of all.'

Surprised, he frowned. 'How do you mean, Princess?'

'You don't have to marry me.'

'I believe you are aware of the political incentive to do so.'

'Political incentive?' To both his shock and irritation Halina looked scornful. 'Do you really think my father will support your claim to the throne?'

Zayed felt a chill spread through his body. 'Do you know something I do not, Princess Halina?'

'No, only that I have never trusted my father wholly. He isn't a cruel man, but his own reputation and comfort comes above everyone else's.'

'I suppose it is a risk I am willing to take.'

'And what of Olivia?'

Zayed tensed. 'What of her?'

Halina cocked her head, her soft brown gaze moving over him slowly. 'Does she not matter at all?'

Zayed said nothing, although everything in him wanted to protest. Shout.

She matters. Of course she matters.

'We are not here to discuss Olivia,' he answered, his tone repressive.

'No,' Halina said slowly. 'We are not.' She was still gazing at him, her expression hard and assessing. 'We are here to discuss our possible marriage.'

'Yes.'

'And the truth is, Prince Zayed, I cannot marry you. I will not.'

Zayed stared at her in shock. 'What?'

'I'm not going to marry you,' Halina stated again, shrugging. 'I'm sorry if it is a disappointment.'

'Your father...'

'My father wants me to marry you. He wants to tidy away my mistake. But he cannot force me.' She lifted her chin. 'No matter what.'

Zayed paused for a moment, aware of what a risk she was taking. Hassan would be furious; he would likely send her away to a remote palace in the desert, never to be seen in society again. He felt a reluctant admiration for the Princess, and underneath another emotion, damning in its intensity. He felt relief.

He didn't want to marry Halina. Whether she was pregnant or not, whether she was willing or not, he didn't want her. He wanted Olivia.

'May I ask why you have come to this decision?' Zayed asked.

'Yes, it is quite simple.' Halina's gaze met his with an unspoken challenge. 'I will not marry a man who is in love with someone else.'

Zayed was too shocked to hide his reaction. *In love...?* 'I don't...' he began, and then stopped. He couldn't deny it. He'd been trying to for days, cutting himself off from Olivia and all that she meant to him because it was necessary for his country. For his rule.

Now Halina tilted her head and gave him a mocking look. 'I'm glad you didn't bother denying it. That does you credit.'

Her audacity surprised and somewhat amused

him. 'What I feel for Olivia has nothing to do with our potential alliance.'

'I'm afraid it does. Because, like I said, I don't wish to marry a man who is in love with someone else, especially when I am pregnant with another man's child.'

'Do you love him?' Zayed asked. He felt nothing either way for Halina and her child—no jealousy, no anger, no interest.

'No,' she answered after a pause. 'But with my child and your love of Olivia our marriage would be both a battle and a breeding ground for resentment.'

'It wouldn't have to be,' Zayed said, but even he sounded unconvinced. The picture Halina was painting was bleak. But what choice did he have?

'Do you know what I think?' Halina said, and Zayed wasn't sure he wanted to know. 'I think you're using your sense of duty as a big, fat excuse.'

'*What?*' The breath whooshed out of Zayed's lungs as he stared at her in mounting fury. 'My father and brother died in the war against Malouf. They were assassinated. I *watched* them die. For the last ten years—' He broke off, struggling with the tidal wave of emotion he felt. 'For the last ten years,' he resumed, 'I have dedicated my life, everything I have, to serving their country and protecting their memory.'

Halina's face softened. 'Prince Zayed, I'm not trying to diminish what happened to your family, or what you've done for them. Of course I'm not. You have suffered and worked tremendously for the good of your country, of your people.'

Zayed nodded, his jaw tight, pain flickering at his temples.

'What I'm saying,' Halina continued steadily, refusing to be cowed, 'is that I believe you are using your sense of duty as a way to get out of being with Olivia.'

'Why,' Zayed demanded, 'would I do that?'

'Because you're scared.'

He stiffened in outrage. He had never been called a coward in his life before this slip of a woman had dared to do so—and over what? '*Scared*? Of what?'

'Of love. Of risking everything for another person. Of fighting for another person, and not just a cause. Of putting yourself out there, of getting hurt.' The smile she gave him was whimsical and a little sad. 'Take your pick.'

Zayed was unable to speak…to think…because in that devastating moment he knew she was right. He *was* scared. He'd lost people he'd loved so he'd never wanted to love again. Seeing Olivia after the snake had bitten her had been utterly terrifying, and he'd done his best to distance himself from her both physically and emotionally—for his own sake. Because he was scared. Because he was a coward.

'Princess Halina, I still need your father's support.'

'I have to believe that there are other ways of getting it, or other countries who can come to your aid. Don't make that your reason, Prince Zayed, not when it is merely an excuse.'

'Plenty of rulers have chosen to marry out of duty,' Zayed snapped.

Halina smiled. 'Then don't be one of them.'

'And what about you? What will you do?'

Halina shrugged, not meeting his gaze. 'I am not your concern, Prince Zayed. Olivia is.'

Zayed's mind was in a ferment all afternoon as he paced his room at the palace, his thoughts going round in an endless, useless loop. He loved Olivia. He was afraid to love her. Afraid, too, to follow his own heart. What if it left his country in an even worse place, his people even more oppressed? Could he possibly be so selfish?

He stood at the window and watched the sun set over the desert, turning sand and sky to blazing gold. He had a sudden, piercing memory of Olivia in the desert, tending to the tribespeople, showing love and gentleness to all she encountered.

She would make a wonderful queen. She was

his wife and his people had already accepted her. Why had he not been able to see that before in all its breath-taking clarity? He'd been so consumed with the alliance with Hassan, but in a sudden second of absolute certainty he realised that he should never have counted on that at all. He needed to win his people over, his country over, not depend on someone's support from the outside. Just as he needed to win Olivia.

He turned from the room, determined, desperate to see her. To tell her all that was in his heart and mind. He found his way to the staff quarters where she normally slept, saw the small, spartan chamber she'd called her own and felt his heart rend all over again. She'd had so little here, yet she'd been so grateful. And she'd asked for nothing from him…but his love.

He spun away from the room and hurried downstairs, needing to find her. 'Where is Olivia?' he asked the first member of the palace staff he came across, a startled-looking man in royal livery. 'Where is Miss Taylor?'

'Miss Taylor?' The man shook his head. 'She is gone. She took a car to the airport an hour ago.'

CHAPTER FIFTEEN

Three months later

PARIS WAS BEAUTIFUL in the autumn. From her apartment on the Ile de la Cité, Olivia could see the winding green of the river, the leaves of the trees alongside now starting to turn red and gold.

She'd been in Paris for three months, having left her heart back in Abkar with Zayed, but she was doing her best to live her life without it. Without him.

Upon arriving she'd stayed with her godmother, who had been surprisingly glad to see her. Olivia had been grateful to renew the acquaintance, and her godmother had also provided a useful contact to enable her to get a job in translation for a large corporation. Within a few weeks Olivia had both a job and an apartment and was cultivating a small group of friends from work. This was the life she had dreamed of, yet it felt so terribly empty.

She had heard nothing from Zayed, no word of an annulment or divorce, even, so bizarrely they were still married. She'd avoided tabloids and gossip magazines, not wanting to read of his resumed betrothal to Halina, and when her friend had contacted her on social media Olivia had guiltily ignored her. She wasn't ready yet. Everything still felt raw and fragile. But she would get there. The last few months, first with Zayed and now in Paris, had showed her how strong she was, and she depended on that strength now. A broken heart could mend. A shattered life could be rebuilt.

She had heard news of Kalidar; it was impossible to ignore when it made the headlines. The military had staged a coup and asked Zayed to return as their leader. Apparently, they had been growing tired of Malouf's ill treatment. Bloody skirmishes had followed, with Malouf making a desperate last stand, but a week ago Zayed had ridden into the capital city of Arjah, triumphant and regal. He'd had Malouf imprisoned and tried for war crimes as well as the murder of his family. In a few weeks he was finally going to be crowned King of Kalidar.

Olivia was happy for him. He'd finally achieved all he'd been striving for for so long. All he deserved. She wondered if his marriage to Halina would go ahead, but she knew it didn't matter anyway. Zayed hadn't loved her. Hadn't chosen her. Whether he married Halina or not was irrelevant.

And she needed to get on with her life. With a weary sigh Olivia reached for her bag and slung it over her shoulder. She enjoyed the translation work she did, but she couldn't see herself doing it for ever. The future yawned ahead of her, as bleak and endless as the desert sands.

She needed to stop thinking like that. And to stop thinking about the desert, or Kalidar, or anything to do with Zayed. Anything could trigger memories of their time together—a hard blue sky, the taste of anise, the whisper of silk. All of it brought the days and nights she'd spent with him, falling in love with him, rushing back.

Olivia walked down the four narrow flights of stairs to the street, opening the front door of her building to a crisp autumn day…and Zayed.

She stared at him in disbelief, blinking several times as if she thought he might vanish, a desert mirage right here in the middle of Paris.

'Hello, Olivia.'

Still she stared. He wore a navy-blue business suit, his dark hair brushed back from his bronzed face, his grey-green eyes sparkling as he gave her a smile that was both wry and tender.

'What…?' Her voice was hoarse. 'What are you doing here?'

'Looking for you.'

The frail hope that had been unfurling inside her withered before it had had the barest chance to bloom. 'You want a divorce,' she said woodenly. After all this time, it shouldn't hurt, but even now it felt as if he were plunging a careless fist into her chest and yanking her heart out. Her last tie to him would be cleanly severed.

'A divorce?' Zayed shook his head. 'No, Olivia, I don't want a divorce.'

'But Princess Halina…?'

'Have you not heard from her?'

Olivia bit her lip and shook her head. 'I haven't.'

'And nor have I. Princess Halina refused to marry me, back when we were both in Abkar.'

'Refused,' Olivia repeated. Her mind was whirling. 'That must have been disappointing.' Had he come to her as second best? Once she would have accepted being the runner up, a last resort. She would have been grateful. But Zayed, funnily enough, had shown her that she was worth more. That she deserved more. Too bad he hadn't realised it.

'It was surprising,' Zayed allowed. 'But not disappointing. What I felt most of all, *habibi*, was relief. Because the only woman I want to be married to is my wife.'

Olivia registered the term distantly. She still

couldn't believe what he was saying, what he was implying.

'It's been three months, Zayed, and I haven't heard a word from you.'

'I know.' He took a measured breath. 'A few days after I last saw you, Malouf's military staged a coup. There was bloodshed and violence; I could not leave my country.'

'I know that. I read about it in the news. But since then...not even a message...?' She shook her head, hating that it had come to this, that part of her, even now, wanted to accept whatever he was offering. How little he was offering.

'I had to find you first,' Zayed replied steadily. 'And, the truth is, I wanted to give you some time.'

'Time?'

'To consider what you really want. I know, Olivia, that you've never really lived on your own. You never had a chance to discover what you were truly capable of. I wanted to give you that chance, as well as some emotional distance from what we experienced. So we could both discover if what we felt was real and lasting.'

'What we felt.' Olivia hitched her bag higher on her shoulder, afraid to hope. 'What is it you feel, Zayed?'

There was no hesitation in his voice as he answered. 'I love you. I've loved you for a long time now. The seeds were planted that first night.'

Why was she so afraid to believe? 'But you left me,' Olivia whispered. 'When I was so ill…'

'That's when I realised I loved you. I was terrified, Olivia, of losing you. Terrified, selfishly, for myself and the pain I would feel. That's why I started to keep my distance, because I was a coward.' He shook his head, his features pinched with regret. 'But I realised—and Princess Halina helped me—that I didn't want to be that kind of coward. Loving you has brought out the best in me, and I want to be the kind of man who loves. Who isn't afraid to love. And I love you, quite desperately. Very deeply. But…' His gaze was steady on her, a shadow of vulnerability in his mossy eyes. 'The question is, do you love me? Will you remain as my wife, Olivia, and as my Queen?'

Olivia took a deep breath, trying to sift through all her emotions. She drew another breath and her face crumpled.

'Olivia!' Zayed exclaimed, her name torn from his lips, then she was in his arms, her face buried in his shoulder, his hands stroking her hair. '*Habibi*, I'm so sorry for hurting you. I wanted to give you your freedom, but perhaps I should have come sooner.'

'No.' Olivia took several gulping breaths before she felt able to continue. 'No, it's just... I didn't think I'd ever see you again. And I love you so much, Zayed. It felt as if it was tearing me apart.'

'I know how that feels, and I wouldn't wish it on anyone. But we are together now, Olivia, and I promise you, I swear on my life, I will never hurt you. That is my solemn vow.'

Olivia let out a little gurgle of tearful laughter as she eased away from him. 'Do you know, that was the first thing you said to me when you came through the window? That you wouldn't hurt me, and it was your solemn vow.'

'And I'm sorry for the times I did hurt you,' Zayed said seriously. 'Emotionally.'

'Oh, Zayed...'

'I meant it then and I mean it even more now,' Zayed told her. 'I love you with my life, Olivia, my soul. I want you by my side, in my bed, hand in hand through everything.'

'I want that too,' Olivia whispered, her eyes shining with tears of pure happiness. 'So much.'

A smile of both relief and joy split Zayed's face and he drew her towards him for a deep and lingering kiss.

'Then I am the happiest man on earth right now.'

'And I,' Olivia answered, kissing him back, 'am the happiest woman.'

Three months later

Bells rang throughout the capital city of Arjah in celebration of the wedding of Kalidar's new King and Queen. Zayed listened to the joyful peals and felt happiness swell in his heart. He could not ask for more from his people, from his country, from his wife.

He turned to Olivia, dressed in a white lace dress and veil, her dark hair pulled back in a low chignon. She looked radiant, her eyes sparkling with happiness, her mouth curved with laughter.

'At least I understood that ceremony,' she teased as she came towards him.

Zayed grinned back at her. 'It was only a blessing, rather than a proper marriage. We can't be married twice.'

'Once is enough for me.' She took his hand and laid her head against his shoulder. 'I couldn't ask for more.'

'I was thinking the same thing.'

The last three months of peace and prosperity in Kalidar had brought Zayed immense satisfaction. Leaders around the world had offered their support, and he'd slowly but surely set about righting ten years of wrongs, building up his city and his people. His father, his family, would have been proud, he hoped. He felt a peace deep inside him that had been absent this long decade; their memories had been honoured, their deaths avenged.

Below them, in the courtyard in front of the palace, a cry rose up.

'I think they want us to go out on the balcony,' Olivia said with a smile.

'Then so we must.' Drawing her by the hand, Zayed stepped out onto the balcony with his bride. The cheers were deafening as the people filling the square called out their approval. Zayed glanced at Olivia and saw the love that suffused her face, felt its answer in himself. No, he could not ask for more. He had absolutely everything he wanted in the woman by his side.

Zayed and Olivia waved at the crowd, both of them smiling, their hearts full of happiness as they gazed out at their shining city.

* * * * *

If you enjoyed
DESERT PRINCE'S STOLEN BRIDE
by Kate Hewitt,
why not explore these other
CONVENIENTLY WED! stories?

HIS MERCILESS MARRIAGE BARGAIN
by Jane Porter
BOUGHT WITH THE ITALIAN'S RING
by Tara Pammi
BOUND TO THE SICILIAN'S BED
by Sharon Kendrick
IMPRISONED BY THE GREEK'S RING
by Caitlin Crews

Available now!

Get 2 Free Books,
Plus 2 Free Gifts—
just for trying the
Reader Service!

HARLEQUIN *Romance*

YES! Please send me 2 FREE Harlequin® Romance Larger-Print novels and my 2 FREE gifts (gifts are worth about $10 retail). After receiving them, if I don't wish to receive any more books, I can return the shipping statement marked "cancel." If I don't cancel, I will receive 4 brand-new novels every month and be billed just $5.34 per book in the U.S. or $5.74 per book in Canada. That's a savings of at least 15% off the cover price! It's quite a bargain! Shipping and handling is just 50¢ per book in the U.S. and 75¢ per book in Canada*. I understand that accepting the 2 free books and gifts places me under no obligation to buy anything. I can always return a shipment and cancel at any time. The free books and gifts are mine to keep no matter what I decide.

119/319 HDN GMWL

Name	(PLEASE PRINT)

Address	Apt. #

City	State/Prov.	Zip/Postal Code

Signature (if under 18, a parent or guardian must sign)

Mail to the **Reader Service:**
IN U.S.A.: P.O. Box 1341, Buffalo, NY 14240-8531
IN CANADA: P.O. Box 603, Fort Erie, Ontario L2A 5X3
Want to try two free books from another line?
Call 1-800-873-8635 or visit www.ReaderService.com.

*Terms and prices subject to change without notice. Prices do not include applicable taxes. Sales tax applicable in N.Y. Canadian residents will be charged applicable taxes. Offer not valid in Quebec. This offer is limited to one order per household. Books received may not be as shown. Not valid for current subscribers to Harlequin Romance Larger-Print books. All orders subject to approval. Credit or debit balances in a customer's account(s) may be offset by any other outstanding balance owed by or to the customer. Please allow 4 to 6 weeks for delivery. Offer available while quantities last.

Your Privacy—The Reader Service is committed to protecting your privacy. Our Privacy Policy is available online at www.ReaderService.com or upon request from the Reader Service.

We make a portion of our mailing list available to reputable third parties that offer products we believe may interest you. If you prefer that we not exchange your name with third parties, or if you wish to clarify or modify your communication preferences, please visit us at www.ReaderService.com/consumerchoice or write to us at Reader Service Preference Service, P.O. Box 9062, Buffalo, NY 14240-9062. Include your complete name and address.

HRLP17R3

Get 2 Free Books,
<u>Plus</u> 2 Free Gifts –
just for trying the *Reader Service!*

YES! Please send me 2 FREE novels from the Essential Romance or Essential Suspense Collection and my 2 FREE gifts (gifts are worth about $10 retail). After receiving them, if I don't wish to receive any more books, I can return the shipping statement marked "cancel." If I don't cancel, I will receive 4 brand-new novels every month and be billed just $6.74 each in the U.S. or $7.24 each in Canada. That's a savings of at least 16% off the cover price. It's quite a bargain! Shipping and handling is just 50¢ per book in the U.S. and 75¢ per book in Canada*. I understand that accepting the 2 free books and gifts places me under no obligation to buy anything. I can always return a shipment and cancel at any time. The free books and gifts are mine to keep no matter what I decide.

Please check one: ☐ Essential Romance   ☐ Essential Suspense
                         194/394 MDN GMWR   191/391 MDN GMWR

Name _____ (PLEASE PRINT) _____

Address _____ Apt. # _____

City _____ State/Prov. _____ Zip/Postal Code _____

Signature (if under 18, a parent or guardian must sign) _____

Mail to the **Reader Service:**
IN U.S.A.: P.O. Box 1341, Buffalo, NY 14240-8531
IN CANADA: P.O. Box 603, Fort Erie, Ontario L2A 5X3

Want to try two free books from another line?
Call 1-800-873-8635 or visit www.ReaderService.com.

*Terms and prices subject to change without notice. Prices do not include applicable taxes. Sales tax applicable in NY. Canadian residents will be charged applicable taxes. Offer not valid in Quebec. This offer is limited to one order per household. Books received may not be as shown. Not valid for current subscribers to the Essential Romance or Essential Suspense Collection. All orders subject to approval. Credit or debit balances in a customer's account(s) may be offset by any other outstanding balance owed by or to the customer. Please allow 4 to 6 weeks for delivery. Offer available while quantities last.

Your Privacy—The Reader Service is committed to protecting your privacy. Our Privacy Policy is available online at www.ReaderService.com or upon request from the Reader Service.

We make a portion of our mailing list available to reputable third parties that offer products we believe may interest you. If you prefer that we not exchange your name with third parties, or if you wish to clarify or modify your communication preferences, please visit us at www.ReaderService.com/consumerschoice or write to us at Reader Service Preference Service, P.O. Box 9062, Buffalo, NY 14240-9062. Include your complete name and address.

STRS17R2

HOME on the RANCH

YES! Please send me the **Home on the Ranch Collection** in Larger Print. This collection begins with 3 FREE books and 2 FREE gifts in the first shipment. Along with my 3 free books, I'll also get the next 4 books from the Home on the Ranch Collection, in LARGER PRINT, which I may either return and owe nothing, or keep for the low price of $5.24 U.S./ $5.89 CDN each plus $2.99 for shipping and handling per shipment*. If I decide to continue, about once a month for 8 months I will get 6 or 7 more books, but will only need to pay for 4. That means 2 or 3 books in every shipment will be FREE! If I decide to keep the entire collection, I'll have paid for only 32 books because 19 books are FREE! I understand that accepting the 3 free books and gifts places me under no obligation to buy anything. I can always return a shipment and cancel at any time. My free books and gifts are mine to keep no matter what I decide.

268 HCN 3760 468 HCN 3760

Name	(PLEASE PRINT)
Address	Apt. #
City	State/Prov.	Zip/Postal Code

Signature (if under 18, a parent or guardian must sign)

Mail to the **Reader Service:**
IN U.S.A.: P.O. Box 1867, Buffalo, NY. 14240-1867
IN CANADA: P.O. Box 609, Fort Erie, Ontario L2A 5X3

* Terms and prices subject to change without notice. Prices do not include applicable taxes. Sales tax applicable in NY. Canadian residents will be charged applicable taxes. This offer is limited to one order per household. All orders subject to approval. Credit or debit balances in a customer's account(s) may be offset by any other outstanding balance owed by or to the customer. Please allow 3 to 4 weeks for delivery. Offer available while quantities last. Offer not available to Quebec residents.

Your Privacy—The Reader Service is committed to protecting your privacy. Our Privacy Policy is available online at www.ReaderService.com or upon request from the Reader Service.

We make a portion of our mailing list available to reputable third parties that offer products we believe may interest you. If you prefer that we not exchange your name with third parties, or if you wish to clarify or modify your communication preferences, please visit us at www.ReaderService.com/consumerchoice or write to us at Reader Service Preference Service, P.O. Box 9062, Buffalo, NY. 14240-9062. Include your complete name and address.

HRCBPA18

READERSERVICE.COM

Manage your account online!

- Review your order history
- Manage your payments
- Update your address

> ### We've designed the Reader Service website just for you.

Enjoy all the features!

- Discover new series available to you, and read excerpts from any series.
- Respond to mailings and special monthly offers.
- Browse the Bonus Bucks catalog and online-only exculsives.
- Share your feedback.

Visit us at:

ReaderService.com

RS16R